The Diary Of A Former

Sex Addict

Part 2

by:

PORSCHE DAY

Thick Nubian Goddess

ISBN 978-0-578-93924-7

Ordering Information: *For information about special discounts available for bulk purchases, sales promotions, fund-raising and educational needs, contact the Author at the above email.*

I would like to give Special Thanks to
Alecia Brown, Aaron Clark, Jasmine Day, C.J. Harris, Rasheb Knight, OGW Publishing (Odessa),
and many others that have been there for me through my journey of building my brand.

*I dedicate this book to my parents **Zena Day-Allen** and **Michael Day***

The Meeting

He's huge and he looked like a football player. He's the man? Tiffany thought to herself. The boy is thirteen! Tiffany played it cool and sat down when Hazel told them to. "state your business." Jay tells them. He sounds like a grown ass man. I can't believe this! In the car they were talking about all the people he's killed and all the houses he's burned down. "I'm Buffalo, these are my brothers."

"Nigga I know who y'all small timers are! State ya business or roll!"

"We want to do business with you. We heard you got the best coke. Shit you got the best drugs!"

"I see how you are Buffalo but I can't do business with that child molesting, corny ass pimp Tommy!"

"I'm not doing this with him."

"Oh really? How do you think he's gonna take that?"

"I think you have a problem on your hands." Jay continued.Yup,you see that little twelve year old he has been sneaking around to see ain't no twelve year old. She's undercover."

Buffalo, Mike and Tory all looked at each other. Tory mumbles to himself, "stupid mothafucka."

"Stupid mothafucka indeed, responded Jay. He heard everything. So before we do business take care of your problem. Now who is she? Jay asked, looking over at Tiffany."

Buffalo answered, "This is my girl Tiffany."

"Do you trust her?" Tiffany wanted to yell nigga are you serious! But something told her to stay quiet. Little John was not who she knew anymore. "Yeah I trust her that's why she's here," replied Buffalo."

"Good. You kill Tommy, Tiffany." Jay states.

"What?"

"You heard me. Seduce and kill him. You have twenty four hours. Call Hazel when the deed is done so we can get rid of him properly." "Here" Jay passes Tiffany a forty five. He's fucking crazy! Doesn't he recognize me! Tiffany takes the gun and puts it in her purse. "You sure you want her to do it?" Buffalo asked.

"Y'all can go." Hazel said as she began to escort them out.

In the car Tiffany started sweating bullets. Her thoughts were in overdrive.

Kill Tommy! I mean I do want to beat his ass for hitting Keke. But I was now expected to seduce and kill him! Little John must have gone crazy!

"Tiff, are you cool?" Buffalo asked, interrupting my thoughts.

"What's Jay's deal? Why do you wanna work with him? I mean kill your cousin?" "He wants us to kill your cousin!"

"Tiff he needs to get got he got the cops on us. Plus he won't see it coming from you. Tomorrow, come on to him and take him to the back room. Set it up real sexy. Tonight he thinks we all went out to the casino. Tommy doesn't suspect shit."

Tiffany kept staring at the gun once she got back to Buffalo's room. She was alone with her thoughts. I needed this when I was being raped by Uncle Todd, she said to herself. Buffalo said he's gonna show me how to use it. Tiffany's cell phone rings, it's Mark. "Hello."

"Tiffany boo I love you. I mean I did cheat once since we've been back together but come on I'll do anything you want."

"I'll talk to you later okay? I don't feel like this right now."

"Tiff-" Tiffany hangs up on Mark before he could finish whatever it is he was going to say next. Buffalo comes back into the room. "Alright, I'm gonna show you how to use this." Tiffany takes out the gun and Buffalo explains the forty five to her. It all seemed simple enough.

Janell

Janell couldn't wait to come back to the house to hear what happened with the meeting.

"Tiff you sleep?" Janell knocks on Buffalo's door.

"No. I'm coming." Tiffany slid her way out of Buffalo's strong arms, he slept hard.

Tiffany and Janell went to the dining room for some privacy. "How did it go?"

"We have a big problem."

Janell's face drops "What problem?"

"Tommy has the cops on his ass...that's what Jay told us. They want me to kill Tommy."

"What the fuck Tiffany? What kind of shit is this?"

"That's not even the worst part...Jay is Little John!"

"Hahahaha! Bitch you lying!"

"No but he didn't say anything about knowing me and I did the same. I was scared. He's a killer! He's crazy! We can't say shit about it either Janell. I have to kill Tommy tomorrow."

"Why would Little John do this to you?"

"I think he wants to see if he can trust me."

"You're his sister."

"I don't think it matters anymore Janell. How did you do tonight?"

"I made five hundred!"

"Damn!"

"I missed out on some serious money tonight! Killing Tommy better be worth it."

Saturday

Tiffany just couldn't stop staring at the gun Little John gave her. To take her mind off tonight Tiffany turned the television to MTV Jams. Buffalo and Mike made sure the basement was in order for tonight. That was one less thing she had to worry about. Buffalo told Tiffany he would call her so that she could call Tommy. When Tiffany looked at her cell it was Buffalo right on schedule. "Call." Buffalo hangs up. Tiffany calls Tommy and uses the codes that Buffalo gave her. Tommy is going to leave early with Tiffany from Hicks Street. This is easier than I thought. Janell comes into Buffalo's room with only her panties on. "Do you think I'm getting fat?"

"Shut up Janell! No! Move. I'm watching my videos!" Janell sits down on the bed next to Tiffany. Life almost seemed normal at that moment.

Tiffany was excited to make the money that she missed last night. Some New York dudes came through because Jay sent them to check out the place. They kept tipping Tiffany with fifty dollar bills. Keke wore a lot of makeup to cover up her black eye. The more Tiffany thought about how disgusting Tommy was, the more killing him made sense. Tommy watched Tiffany with lust in his eyes. Tiffany caught his eye a few times and wink at him. You're so dead, she thought to herself.

As planned Tiffany throws on her jacket and signals Tommy to meet her outside. "I'm not gonna lie, I was wanting you the moment I saw you." Tiffany tells Tommy as they drive to Buffalo's house. "I want you too! Your ass is fat!" Tommy rubs on Tiffany's legs the entire ride. "I got something special for you baby! Follow me." Tiffany takes Tommy by the hand and leads him down to the basement. Rose petals covered the bed with wine glasses sitting on the dresser. Tiffany turns on the stereo system. Tommy takes his jacket off and sits on the bed. Tiffany gives him the glass of wine. Instead of joining him, she begins to dance for him seductively, licking her lips, and sucking her fingers. As she is watching Tommy get excited all the memories of being raped started coming back to her. The way Uncle Todd used to look at her made Tiffany sick to her stomach. Todd's lifeless body falling to hers put an end to her misery but it took away the only man who truly loved her. Her father. Tiffany instructed Tommy to get naked for her and lay on the bed of roses. Tommy happily did as he was told. Tiffany starts taking off her lingerie once she gets down to the bottoms she dances down to the floor to get the forty five that's hidden under the bed. "Close your eyes baby!"

"They are!" Tiffany rises up to see if Tommy's eyes are closed. He's so stupid and corny. Tiffany shoots Tommy dick first. He screams in agony but no one can hear him over the music. "You disgusting piece of shit!" Tiffany shoots Tommy eight times in total. The stomach, chest, and head. Buffalo was waiting upstairs the entire time. Once he didn't hear the music anymore he ran down to the basement to see Tiffany still holding the gun and Tommy dead in a bed filled with bloody roses. "Tiff, give me the gun." Tiffany hesitates at first but then hands it to him. Buffalo calls the number that Jay gave him. Tiffany and Buffalo go upstairs. "Go clean yourself up." Tiffany didn't say anything she just did as she was told. In the shower tears flowed down Tiffany's eyes. "Tiffany get it together," she said to herself.

Once Tiffany showered and dressed she went downstairs to see Little John and his crew.

"I need a word in private with your girl." Jay walks over to Tiffany. Tiffany and Jay go upstairs to Buffalo's room. Jay walks up to Tiffany and hugs her. "Tiffany you fuckin' did that shit!"

"Little John!" Tiffany punches her little brother in the face. He grabs his chin to see blood. Tiffany busted his lip. "It's cool sis. I get it! I had to see why you are here. If I could trust you."

"I'm here to make money."

"The hell do you mean make money? I was making weekly deposits to Aunt Pat's house...she got greedy huh. I thought you would be happy to kill a dude like Tommy. Keke is straight up stupid!"

"Does she know who you are?"

"No. All are dead who knew me and where I come from. No one knows shit about me just that I'm the man and running shit."

"The man? Boy, you're thirteen! You don't look it though. You've grown so much. Vanessa is gone with Derrick."

"I know I keep up with y'all. I know Brenda killed Joy."

"What?"

"Shock me too. I know about Mark...he's quite popular with them little white girls. I don't want anyone to know that you're my sister. You work for me and you keep fuckin' with Buffalo. Stay a stripper or whatever. I got plans sis it's me and you. I love you. I got a man inside at the jail. Daddy is still in the hole."

Tiffany felt relieved to hear that her father was ok. Should I tell Little John what dad said about me being his only child? No, it would break his heart if he hasn't already figured it out for himself. Jay gives Tiffany another cell phone. "This is for us only. Keep it hidden. Let's go back downstairs." Tiffany and Jay go back downstairs. Buffalo notices Jay's busted lip. "What the fuck happened?" Jay looked at Tiffany.

"Nothing...we are in business. Come by the garage tomorrow at five in the morning." Jay and his crew leave.

"Tiffany yo what happened up there?" Buffalo couldn't believe Tiffany punched Jay in the house.

"I handled my business. Are y'all leaving Tommy's body in the basement?"

"Naw...they took Tommy and the sheets. Mike and Tory gonna clean up the basement." Don't worry about anything Tiffany."

"One thing though...what happens to Tommy's stable?"

"Dee Dee is gonna run them. Not how Tommy had it. Only one that might ask questions is Keke."

"Yeah. She's the only one who loved his corny ass." Tiffany and Buffalo laughed.

August 1997

After the school year ended I left Aunt Pat's house for good. She wasn't pleased with the fact that Jay stopped sending money to the house. Since she didn't have Uncle Jake taking care of her anymore she had to get a job. Simone got her a night job cleaning office buildings. She hates it but what else could she do? Aunt Pat never went to college or trade school. I knew that this life I chose it wouldn't be wise to stay with Aunt Pat and have her try to take my money. When I left I wrote her letter and left it on the dining room table. Watching her go down hill reminded me of Brenda too much. I hate Brenda and I didn't want to hate Aunt Pat. She was there when no one else was or wanted to be. Jay puts money on Daddy's books. Janell still lives at home and comes to stay with us every weekend happily.

Living with Buffalo has been good. Since he got in with Jay money flows like water. For my birthday he got me a diamond bracelet and stud earrings. Mark still calls my phone. I did go see him last week. We didn't have sex I told him I would think about giving him another chance. For now we are just friends. Keke's dumb ass is pregnant by Tommy. When she found out that Tommy was dead she had a breakdown. She accused Buffalo of murdering him. He allows her to think that to protect me. We told her to get an abortion but she says she keeping her baby in honor of Tommy. Shar left after Tommy's murder. We have eyes on her. She returned back home to Darby with her mother. The rest of the stable including Keke are doing well under Dee Dee. Tommy's children were returned to their mothers. He told them they were worthless now to him. The first baby mom hasn't seen her two sons in three years. Tommy threatened to kill her if she tried to get them. The last one thought it was a dream to see her daughters. When she was kicked out the house Tommy cut her face with a razor. It was a blessing that neither one of them became drug addicts or alcoholics. The best happy ending Tiffany has seen in awhile.

Tiffany was excited to be getting out of philly for a day. Jay took her and Hazel to New York to meet Victor, Triggers connect. Trigger met his demise without Jay's hand in it. One of his cousins found him dead in his bed, having had a heart attack in his sleep. Naturally his soldiers lined up for Jay. Hazel is the only person who knows Tiffany is his sister. That's only because she thought he was interested in Tiffany. Hazel liked that she knew something personal about Jay. He always listened to her badlands stories. Rambo was the driver for their Brooklyn trip. Rambo is the only one with a clean license. For this trip they drove a 1995 green Chevrolet Suburban to fit all of Jay's shipment in one trip.

Victor did his business out of a soul food restaurant. He closed the restaurant early to entertain Jay, Hazel, Rambo, and Tiffany. Victor took a likening to Jay. He liked him better than Trigger. Jay was about everybody eating, not just the boss. He wasn't greedy and there had been some small talk about him having some New York territory. Tiffany never imagined that this was the life her brother wanted. She thought he wanted to be a NFL player or something of that nature not a crime lord.

"Did y'all enjoy the food?" Victor asked.

"Yeah. We need to get back on the road." Jay explains to Victor.

"Jay, relax. You got time my friend. Remember to have a good time in the mist of business. You're young but now is the time to learn patience. Do you want a family one day?"

"I don't know. I don't want anything that can become a weakness."

"Hmmm. I see. One day that may change. One day you're gonna have to put down the crown if you want to make it to my age."

"I just know right now, Vick. But I'll keep all that in mind."

Tiffany sits at the table listening to Victor's words in her head. I never thought about that either. Rambo and Hazel got up and went with Victor's men to check on the shipment.

"When you're ready Jay invest into something more than just the streets."

"I will do that Vick."

Jay gets up from the table and signals Tiffany to join him in checking out the shipment.

Tiffany never saw so much cocaine in her life. If Brenda was here she would overdose and be in cocaine heaven.

Buffalo

Buffalo wasn't feeling all the attention Jay was giving Tiffany. What was he trying to do, take my girl? Why can't I meet the connect? Buffalo paced back and forth around the living room waiting for Tiffany to arrive back home. "Yo Buff you good man?" Mike noticedBuffalo's pacing back and forth. "No…why did Tiffany get to meet the connect? Does he like her? He tryin' to steal her from me?"

"Listen, who cares! We are up now! Don't fuck this up over no bitch! Or I will kill you…Tiffany is straight. She plays her part well."

"You right man. I'm gonna chill out. I love her."

Mike laughs uncontrollably. "Clearly!"

"It's not funny. I do though. I feel like she understands me."

"You sound like a bitch but I hear you." Mike looks out the window to see Tiffany getting out of the Suburban. "Here she comes. Don't act up! We need her to keep doing whatever it is she is doing." Buffalo plops down on his lazy boy.

"Hey y'all!" She walks over and kisses Buffalo on the cheek.

"How was New York?" Buffalo asked as cool as possible.
"Cool. We need to go for a trip. Tory is at the garage making sure y'all shit is set. I'm going to bed."

John

After months of solitary confinement I'm finally back in a cell. During my time in the hole I felt like I was going crazy. I swore Todd's ghost was in there with me laughing at me. I don't regret killing him! However I do regret the consequences behind killing him. You would think there would be some kind of reward for getting rid of scum like Todd.

I have a new cell mate from Philly. He's been telling me about how he's hooked up on the outside with some kingpin named Jay. His whole family is paid while he does this twenty year stretch for Jay. All I'm thinking about is my children. I immediately started writing letters to Tiffany apologizing for my absence. A few weeks later I get a letter from Pat telling me my child is gone. Vanessa is with her real father and Little John is still M.I.A. Jake is gone but money is still being put on my books. An angel is watching over me during my time of need. She told me Joy was stabbed and pushed into an el train. Now that Joy is gone I have to figure out another way to file for a divorce from Brenda. She was supposed to help me with that. So much bad is going on. Pat has not answered any of the phone calls. I asked too much of Pat. I never thought about how much their lives could change too.

"I don't know where my daughter is. My sister-in-law said she's gone." John starts explaining to his cellmate Jerry." "You want me to find her for you? You got a picture I can show my girl when she comes to visit me?"

"Yeah. This is a couple years old."

"Don't worry about it. I'll help you. You're a good man." I just told Jay about you. He said he heard about you. "You killed your daughter's rapist. He put money on ya books."

"He did?"

"Yeah he told me if you need anything let him know. So I know Jay and my girl will help you find your daughter."

Why is this Jay looking out for me? I hope this isn't another threat from Brenda. I don't want to have to kill him too. I'll just play it cool for now until I'm given a reason to take it there.

Jay

Jay took Victor's advice with living life more. He told Tiffany to meet him at the garage so that they could spend brother and sister time together. He contemplated on telling her about how he was responsible for Uncle Jake's death. If I tell her she will blame me for ruining her life. I just can't tell her. When Tiffany arrived at the garage Jay made sure it was all clear. He wanted them to be completely alone. "What are we gonna do?" Tiffany asked Jay.

"I wanted us to be alone and spend some time together."

"I just wanted you to know that I love you and have done everything in my power to protect you. I never wanted you in this life this way. I wanted you to benefit from it."

"I know Little... I mean Jay. I thought you wanted to be an NFL dude or something."

"Ha! That's funny. So my man that's locked up, Jerry...he's Dad's cell mate. Aunt Pat told Dad that you're gone. I'm arranging a ride for you tomorrow morning to see him."

"Who's gonna take me there?"

"Buffalo. I got Dad to put him on the visitor list. You can't tell Dad who I am. I told Buffalo that your dad is looking for you. That's all he needs to know."

"I'm happy I get to see Daddy. I miss him so much. I wish we could go together. Is this why you wanted us to be alone?"

"Yeah. Your boy thinks I like you. His brother told me."

"You don't want me to kill him too do you?"

"Naw. Just keep that in mind. Let's go get some pizza and sit out Penn's Landing."

Tiffany happily agreed. Jay drove this time, so Tiffany was impressed.

The rest of the day with Tiffany was great. Jay felt normal at the moment. He felt like a brother instead of a killer or kingpin drug lord. Jay remembered all the disappointments, the fights between his parents, and sleeping on one bed. He was glad that all those days were behind him, even though he rarely sleeps.

Jay decided to take Tiffany to his house. Of course it's in one of his soldier's family members name, but it's his. He lives in a house in a suburb called Folcroft. It's a one floor single home. The house looks like a family lives there with flowers planted and a rose bush. Jay could tell by Tiffany's facial expressions she was not expecting this. "I get my man to bring his grandma here a few times out of the week. Neighbors think she lives here and that I'm her grandchild. Oh and Hazel."

"What's y'all deal?"

"She's my right hand."

"That's it?"

"Yeah for now. I just found out her age."

"Which is?"

"She's eighteen. Been in these streets since eleven like me. She was born into it."

"Wow. She doesn't know you're a big ass thirteen year old?"

"No, I won't touch her yet either. She is in love with me. She told me but I told her I'm not ready for all that yet."

"I can't believe this is our life. I thought I would never see you again."

"Believe it. Now you know my true resting place. Look around. I got a pool table downstairs in the basement."

Tiffany and Jay played pool while Jay told her a little bit about his life on the street. Tiffany shared with her brother some of her past, from coping with being raped, and Keke going crazy. Their brother and sister time ended well until Jay dropped Tiffany home. Buffalo was sitting on the steps drunk and high. "Hey baby!" Tiffany yells from the car. Buffalo stumbles to get up. "Don't baby me! What the fuck is this shit? Huh Jay?"

"What are you talking about Buffalo?" Tiffany asked. Jay gets out of the car.

"What's up Buffalo, is it something on ya mind?" Jay pulls his thirty eight glock out his Guess Jeans. Tiffany begs her brother to stop. Tory comes out the house and sees that Buffalo is about to fuck up everything. "You want her, you can keep her Jay!" Buffalo yells. Tory grabs Buffalo by the arm. "Are you crazy? Jay he means no disrespect."

Tiffany is standing there in limbo. "Jay, I need to tell him! This shit is out of hand!"

"Tell me what Tiffany? You fuckin' Jay? Huh!" Buffalo breaks free of Tory and walks up to Tiffany. "I'm not fuckin' Jay! He's my brother."

"What?!?"

"Remember I told you my family got split up. I swear I love you Tyreek."

Buffalo sobers up fast. He hugs Tiffany quickly. Then he goes over to Jay. He sees no resemblance but Tiffany did say they all had separate daddies. "Jay man, I'm sorry. I love Tiffany."

Jay puts his glock back in his jeans. "This stays between us. You understand." Jay explains. Buffalo nods and takes Tiffany in the house. Tory and Jay stay out front.

"Jay, you know that was driving my bro crazy. He really thought you was fuckin' her. I kind of figured it was something more to it."

"How so?"

"Keke's face when she saw you last week at Hicks Street. I felt like y'all was connected."

"Keke is off Hicks Street if she wanna do that after the baby is born that's her business. Being a pregnant whore ain't cute." Jay told Tory.

"Alright boss." Tory walks into the house.

Jay gets in his car and drives off.

Visiting Day

When John saw his daughter walk in with a man his heart sunk to the floor. Who is this guy to Tiffany? I know I agreed to putting him on the list but something tells me she's definitely not my little girl anymore. Tiffany ran to her father to jump in his arms but he wasn't so receptive. "Daddy I miss you so much!"

"Tiffany, who is Tyreek to you?"

"He's my boyfriend...please don't be mad."

John sat down at the table and placed his head in his arms.

"Sir it's nice meeting you. I have been taking care of Tiffany. I know y'all fell on hard times." The more Buffalo talked the angrier John was getting. "I failed as a father! This is not supposed to be your life!"

"Daddy I'm okay. I had to leave Aunt Pat's house. Daddy don't be like this!"

She was turning into Brenda, he thought."

"All I did was try to protect my children. Protect you. I'm glad you're safe overall."

John hugged his daughter tight. He shook Buffalo's hand. John realized that acting out may turn Tiffany away so he made the choice to accept that it is what it is. There wasn't anything he could do about it. Because of Brenda none of his family would take Tiffany in. They all turned their backs on John once again. The only thing keeping him from completely going under is Tiffany.

"Daddy, I'm learning how to drive!"

"Really? How's that working out?"

"Sir she can't park." Buffalo chimes in.

"Shut up! I will get it before it gets too cold out. I want my license."

"You will get it. How's school?"

"I dropped out…please don't be mad. I will go back later. I promise Daddy!"

John again is cautious with his words. He feels helpless but has no choice but to abide by the life that has been laid out to them. "If you decide to work I understand. But I ask that you bring me a high school diploma or GED. Just no grand babies."

"Okay, Daddy."

Tiffany, Buffalo, and John made the best out of the visit. Avoiding discussions about Brenda or Pat. Even though they desperately wanted to. John wanted to ask Tiffany where she was working or living, but something just kept saying to him that certain things are best kept unsaid. He noticed all the diamonds Tiffany was wearing. She wore makeup and had her nails done.

"Daddy I promise I'm safe. Don't worry about me while you're here."

The Set Up March 1998

Brenda

After Brenda murdered her ex-best friend cold heartedly she ran back to New York until things cooled off, but that was months ago. Star once again welcomed her with open arms despite the fact that she got Zora locked up for the rest of summer in Philadelphia. To them that's just how it was. Victor however was not having it. Brenda snorted up his shipment and spent all their money. Victor told Star that she could only stay for a month then it's back to Philly she goes. Brenda was a hazard to the business and family. Star informed Brenda that she could only stay one more week and that made Brenda angry. How dare Victor! Who does he think he is? Brenda decided to push up on Victor because she needed him. She knew he didn't need her plus her welcome at this point on Victor's end was done.

"Vick...can I talk to you for a minute?" Brenda was laying on the couch of Star and Victor's living room. Brenda had on a black half shirt and grey sweatpants.

Victor looked at Brenda curious to what the hell she had to ask him about? More coke?

"What Brenda? You ain't staying longer just so you know. One more week."

Brenda crawls to Victor from the couch on to the floor. "Aw baby don't be like that...ya know? Ha! I need a favor." Brenda grabs at Victor's dress pants. His eyes roll back in his head. "What favor Brenda?"

"You got anybody on the inside? I need John gone!" Brenda unzips Victor's pants and takes his penis out. She starts massaging it until it's fully erected. Brenda begins giving Victor head. Victor almost fell to the floor because of the sensation of Brenda's mouth. She allows him to sit on the couch and proceeds to finish sucking him off. Victor climaxes in Brenda's mouth. "I may have a few men. You know that you can stay as long as you want. Do you need anything?" Brenda gets off her knees and laughs. "Yeah, make sure that John is dead. I want that bitch bloody dead."

Nobody is gonna get in my way of my revenge, Brenda is deep in her thoughts. Thinking back on how she killed Joy for all her lies and her own daughter seducing her uncle. They are all gonna pay Todd. After I get John out the way I will go move down south with Mama. Tiffany, Little John, and Vanessa can go to hell!

Victor stares at Brenda wondering what thoughts go on in that coked up head of hers.

"Brenda I'm going to clean myself up before Star and Zora come back."

"Alright you do what you gotta. I'll be in my room." Brenda goes upstairs to call Mabel. She hasn't spoken to her mother since John killed Rufus.

"Hello."

"Hey Ma..."

"Brenda, I'm not sending you any money!"

"I was just calling to tell you I may be coming down there soon."

"You will? That's great. You're gonna put the house up for sale?"

"I don't know about that part yet. But I'm thinking about it."

"Alright I'm glad you're coming to your senses." Brenda and Mabel hang up. I don't think I wanna put the house up. I'm sure I can come up with a plan to keep it. I wouldn't even have it if it wasn't for Uncle Sunny paying my bills.

Brenda could hear Star and Zora downstairs. She waited until she heard Victor's voice joining in on their conversation before going down. I don't need any suspicions. Brenda wraps her hair with a scarf to make it look like she was in her room sleeping off a high as usual.

"Hey y'all!" Brenda greets Star and Zora.

The Set Up

John

I think I'm going crazy either that or I'm right about these two Hispanic dudes following me around. I noticed the bald guy when I was in the shower the other day staring at me. I haven't been in no beefs. I told Jerry about it this morning. He said he was going to put a couple guys on them. Jay's guys said they work for Victor. I don't know anyone named Victor! It must be a mistake. Or are they associated with Rufus? I really didn't know a lot of Brenda's family.

"Yeah, Victor from Brooklyn. He moves major weight. I think Jay knows him."

"So is he protected? If Jay knows him?"

"I'll find out by tonight. Jay would've told me unless it's beef and a part of Jay's crew."

"Alright…but why beef?"

Jerry shrugs his shoulders.

John stayed in his cell thinking about the outcomes of this 'beef.' How did I get myself in this bullshit? He's paying for my books? I wanted to ask Tiffany if she knows anything about this since she is definitely with a street guy. How is this my life? John pulls out his picture of Tiffany, Little John, and Vanessa. I remember when Brenda gave birth to Vanessa, I saw her innocent pale face but I knew she wasn't my daughter. The same when Little John was born I mean at first I did think I had a John Junior. Until I saw her at the bar with this big football player looking dude with the same face as my son. If it wasn't for a tip that I know was Joy I would've never known my son was not my son. Not a day that went by I didn't secretly want to just stab Brenda to death in the heart. The way she did me. I'm too deep now. I don't know what's at stake with these guys but I know I have to go with it.

The Set Up

Jay

Jay is sitting in his office at the garage furious at the message he just received. Jerry's girlfriend called Hazel to find out if there is Hispanic protection from Victor. "Jerry said they are following around his cellmate John. He wanted to know if it was beef or protection."

"Why would Victor send men out on my people? Is he trying to set me up? Who tryna move in? Any new independents?"

"Naw Jay. But if he wanted a war, why would he start from jail? No one was beefing on the streets.Who is this John anyway? I know you sent Rambo to put money on his books."

Jay looked at Hazel, should I tell her that's my father? I mean can I truly trust Hazel?

This shit does not add up. I don't want to make a move on them and fuck up my connect with Victor. "It doesn't add up Hazel.I'm gonna call Victor." Jay pulls out his second cell phone to call Victor. "Aye my boy!"

"What's going on man? You got eyes on my man in the cut?"

"Ya man in the cut?"

"Yeah. Two dudes on my man in the cut."

"I didn't know that was ya man. I'm on it."

"Was it a beef?"

"Naw not on me. A favor...let's meet at half point tomorrow at noon."

"Half point it is." Jay hangs up.

"Get word to Jerry girl that it's off."

"You got a meeting now?"

"Yeah...I'm gonna get to the bottom of this shit. Something ain't right."

Hazel left out to do as she's told.

John

It feels like Jerry has been gone forever. Where is he? I hope nobody caught him. Jerry came back to the cell. John got up from the bed anticipating bad news. "Boss said everything is everything. You ain't got no problems."

"You sure?"

"Yeah. Jay said it's all good...when he says that it really is."

"How do you know Jay? I mean how come you're so loyal?"

"I've been out here on these streets since shit... I don't know. I was rolling with Skip but he was foul and Jay peeped it. After that we all been straight."

"How old are you Jerry?"

"I'm twenty one."

"Do you think of what would have happened if you never got caught up?"

"Naw, John...I've been deep in this it's what we do and Jay has been straight and good to all his soldiers like he said he would. How many niggas you know on some honor shit?"

John sat back down on the bed and thought about what Jerry said. This Jay has a lot of eyes and ears. He brought Tiffany to see me. Jerry is twenty one and is in here doing time happily in honor of Jay.

"Not many apparently...thanks for that Jerry."

"We all we got!" Jerry leans in and hugs John.

The Halfway Point

Jay stood outside the rental Rambo purchased for this meeting with Victor. Rambo's job was to drive and stay in the car for meetings unless Jay gave the signal. Jay is heavy in his thoughts, I don't know what the fuck is going on! If it's war then my soldiers are ready. Victor greets Jay with open arms but Jay isn't having it. The two shake hands instead. "Jay…look I didn't know that was ya man. I mean how is he your man? I thought he was in on the killing of an alleged rapist?"

"How do you know what he is in for? Who are you talking to the feds?" Jay reaches for his gun in his jeans. "Calm down Jay. I know his wife, she's my long-time woman's cousin."

Jay is heated. Brenda is trying to kill Dad? What the fuck is she out here telling people? So we have a family in New York? Of course Brenda would keep that hidden for her own personal needs.

"That bitch…" Jay whispers to himself.

"Jay…what is he to you? Why do you care?"

"The question is why do you believe a filthy slut ass crack head?"

"You know Brenda?"

"I know that she's lying to you and was about to cause a war."

Victor could see the anger in Jay's face. Who is he to Brenda and John? No couldn't be…

"Your Little John? Your Brenda's son! Oh my God! She thinks you're some punk running under a kingpin!"

Victor pulls out a Newport from his trench coat.

"My name is Jay. Why are you fuckin' with her?"

"I'm not officially. I was just doing a favor for a favor…she told a convincing story that Tiffany seduced her brother and John was jealous of Todd. I'm sorry Jay. I let her get the best of my better judgment. I told her she could stay longer."

"Stay? She's in New York at your house? Now that you know that's my man, how are you gonna play it?"

Victor takes a drag of his cigarette. "How do you want to play it Jay? You're one of my biggest players. We make a lot of money together. I don't want to fuck it up."

"I'll think of something for dearest Brenda. Until then say nothing to her about it, keep her comfortable."

"You never call her mom? I'm not even sure if I want in on this."

"She's no one's mother and Victor, your hands are clean. Wait for my call."

Victor nods his head, the two part ways. Jay gets back in the car. Rambo looks to Jay waiting for a command. "Yo boss, what's the move?"

"No war."

"No war?" Rambo looked confused. He was sure Jay was gonna come back to the car saying to strap up.

"You heard me nigga no WAR!" He smacks Rambo upside his head. Damn this dude bitch one day about work now he wanna war. How can I get Brenda out of the picture for good? She's out of control. I can't believe Brenda is out here setting up murders. Now I see where I get it from. I don't want to kill her but I do want to send a message. Should I tell Tiffany? She would want Brenda dead for sure. This shit is personal. Brenda is fuckin' with my connect, my money, and my family.

When Jay got back to Philly he decided to tell his sister what was going on. No need to have her in the dark. He sent for Tiffany to be at the garage before he got there. Tiffany was sitting with Hazel. Hazel thinks that Jay is the big brother of Tiffany. Tiffany knows not to correct Hazel's assumptions. Tiffany sees Jay watching them in the doorway. "Yo! We got business so Hazel you can sit this one out. I will need you to holla at Rambo down the way. He said Mickey is fuckin' up the count." Hazel got up from the leather chair, said her goodbyes to Tiffany and kissed her on the cheek. Once the door closes Tiffany turns to Jay awaiting this 'business' situation. Jay sits down in his chair and puts his leg up on the desk. "We have a personal matter. Brenda put a hit out on Dad through my connection who I just found out is our cousin! I didn't admit to being her son and he know that's just code"

"What! How do you know she's trying to have Daddy killed?"

"Jerry sent word. Dad noticed he was being watched."

"That bitch is dead!"

"Hold on Tiff. We can't kill her but we can scare her. Victor doesn't want parts but he's gonna have to play a part in order for this to work."

"What's the move?"

"First we burn down our house."

Tiffany rolled her eyes. This nigga is always talking about burning down something.

"Don't look at me like that Tiffany. We gotta take everything from her."

"I get it...we make that bitch wish she was dead!"

"Exactly."

The Fire

April 1998

Jay told Victor to keep allowing Brenda to believe she had him under her control. Jay purposely did not tell him the full extent of his plans. He knows Victor is going to play his part however Jay wasn't taking any chances. Tiffany couldn't wait to burn down their old house. That house was nothing but bad memories and trauma. The fights, the abuse, the rapes. The only downside of it is it was John's dream home. John put in his hard work and sweat into purchasing that house. Tonight John's dream but his children's nightmare will burn to the ground.

Jay and Tiffany went about this alone. No one in the crew was involved, not even Hazel. Tiffany was hype that Jay let her drive one of the cars. Tiffany parked the car a few blocks away from their childhood home. Tiffany and Jay wore all black down to the gloves, they held hands walking up the block. Tiffany carried the gasoline. Jay broke in from the basement. Tiffany took out her pocket flashlight. They could tell Brenda hadn't been home in months. Before the fire was to begin the brother and sister walked around the house. Tiffany went upstairs and saw herself curled up against the wall crying after John shot Todd. Jay stayed downstairs looking in the cabinets for alcohol. He found vodka and rum cheap too. Perfect for starting a fire. Jay noticed a black over garment laying in the corner of the living room floor. He examines it. Jay remembers Tim reporting to them that he saw Brenda get dressed as a Muslim in the alley the day she killed Joy. Brenda is stupid after all. Tiffany comes downstairs and sees Jay holding the over garment. "Yo this is what she killed Joy in." Jay whispers.

"What?"

"My man said she was wearing this when she stabbed her. I wanna find the knife."

"You think she was dumb enough to bring that home?"

"Yes. She brought this home."

Tiffany and Jay took sections of the house looking for the murder weapon. About twenty minutes in they almost gave up. Tiffany checked the living room closet. Inside the closet she turned on the light to see a little jewelry box. She popped it open and dumped it out. A bunch of fake green jewelry fell out and a pocket knife. Nice try Brenda, Tiffany thought to herself. "This has to

be it. Stupid bitch! Let's light this shit up and be out!"
Tiffany exclaims to Jay. They happily poured out all of
Brenda's alcohol inside the house. Jay turns on the
stove and oven in the upstairs kitchen. Tiffany pours
out the gasoline all over the basement. They didn't start
the fire initially until Jay turned on the basement stove.
Once the flames started they never stopped. By then
Jay and Tiffany were out of sight from the damage they
caused.

Pat

Pat dreaded getting up to do her shift later. I hate working! Online dating sucked tremendously, I can't seem to find another man that is willing to take care of me and my boys. All they want to do is have sex and try to live in my house. The last guy almost had me involved in a robbery! He asked me to drive him to the liquor store and before he got out he put on a black ski mask! Once he got out of my mini van I took off so fast! I'm so done with this shit! I need a rich man. At this point I'm thinking of selling the house to make some money and go live with Aunt Sarah. I'm tired of cleaning toilets and changing trash cans. I don't know where Keke is or Tiffany for that matter. Little John stopped sending money so he must be locked up or I pray not the worst...dead. I almost did turn into Brenda worrying about the children. I was offered a line of coke at the bar I started hanging out at. I just wanted to take my mind off everything!

Pat turns on the television to the five o' clock news. She sees Brenda's house up in flames and the house next door halfway burnt down. Oh my God! 'The Fire was reported last night with no eye witnesses on how the fire started. The family of five next door survived.' I can't believe this bitch! She's lost her mind! She burned her own house down! What is trying to run a scam for insurance money? I know Brenda did this on purpose! I know it! Pat immediately gets on the phone to call Mabel. The phone rings for a long time before Mabel finally picks up. "Hello, Patricia."

"Brenda burned her house!"

"What?"

"She burned down her house! It's on the news! Just like I know she had something to do with Joy's death!"

"Joy's dead?"

"Oh you didn't know?"

"Calm down Patricia! You are making serious accusations!"

"The house is gone Mabel! Joy is gone! It's all Brenda. I know it!"

Mabel takes a long pause on the phone trying to figure out is Brenda truly behind all this? I mean it would explain why she said she is going to come live down here with me. "Mabel you there?"

"Yes…I'm gonna call you back Patricia." They hang up. Pat goes into her drawer, she pulls out a pen and paper.

I need to write to John. He needs to know what's going on. Maybe he has heard from Tiffany.

Brenda

Zora yells for Brenda from the living room to pick up the phone. "Yo Brenda! Pick up the phone, it's Auntie Mabel and she sounds pissed!" Brenda comes out of the kitchen and takes the phone from Zora, she walks to the dining room. "Yes Mom?"

"What the hell is going on up there huh? You burned your house down?"

"I don't know what you are talking about Mom! Burn my house down?"

"Patricia said it's on the news that the house is on fire and that Joy is dead!"

Zora comes into the dining room with a package. She whispers to Brenda "It's for you."

Brenda looks at and says "For me?" Zora walks out the dining room. Brenda opens the package while Mabel is on the other end of the phone cursing her out. Brenda's heart jumps out of her chest. What the fuck! It's the black niqab she wore when she killed Joy. At the bottom of the package is a note that reads *I know what you did!* Brenda is scared out of her mind. "And I told you not to marry that damn John!" Brenda continues on.

"Mom I have to call you back okay!" Brenda hangs up quickly. She goes into the living room where Zora is happily smoking a blunt and watching music videos. "Who sent this?" Brenda asked Zora holding the box.

"The delivery man! Do you want to hit this blunt?"

"Naw! How long before Star and Victor come back?"

"Soon…you good? You look like you saw a ghost."

"Yeah I'm good." Brenda goes upstairs to her room. She looks at the note and niqab. Whoever burned my house down knows I killed Joy. What if they found the knife too? Or what if it's a set up? Someone is fuckin' with me! Bluffing. Why didn't I ditch the evidence like I said I would? Too happy you didn't get caught. You fucked up Brenda. I can't go back to Philly. When Victor gets in here I need answers on John. What if it's John's family who did this? As a retaliation against me! John must be dead then. But how did they find me? Maybe they searched through my shit before burning the house. Yes that's what happened…John's dead. Then why Victor ain't say nothing? He must not have word yet. Well whoever sent this won't find me after tonight. I'm gonna talk to Victor then my ass is going down south with Mabel. Fuck everybody I won.

That Evening

Brenda couldn't wait for Victor to get in the house so she could tell him thank you. Once she heard Star voice Brenda darted down the stairs from her room. Star and Victor just came in from shopping. Something they do almost everyday. Buy new outfits to go out to one of Victor's clubs or restaurants. Star lives the life Brenda desires. Star don't get high like Brenda but to be like Star draped in diamonds what woman wouldn't want that. Victor noticed Brenda seemed off. "Hey cuz you ok?" Victor asked as he lit up his cuban cigar. "I gotta speak with you about that thing we discussed on me leaving." Victor nodded his head. Star hugged Brenda and went upstairs to show Zora her new clothes and shoes. Zora hates shopping and hates even more when her mother comes in with clothes that she has no intentions on wearing.

"What's going on?" Victor asked Brenda.

"Well I take it you did your job cause now they are after me. John's family burned down my house!"

Victor looks at Brenda to figure out how to play it. Clearly Jay has burned down the house. I'm not telling her John is alive and well. Victor nods his head then puffs his cigar.

"Okay, this is the game Brenda. What do you want from me? I did what you asked."

"I need money…I'm leaving tonight. I can't tell anyone where I'm going."

Victor pulls out a bank roll. He gives Brenda five hundred dollars which is more than enough. Brenda takes the money. "Thank you for helping me get my revenge. Y'all looked out for me and got some bomb ass coke. Will you give Star and Zora my goodbyes."

"Sure."

Brenda runs upstairs to her room and grabs her bag. She can hear Zora complaining about her new clothes. Zora doesn't know how good she has it. My children don't even call me 'Mom'. That damn Tiffany ruined our family! Well that's all behind me now. My mom will be happy to see me. I may find a country man to take care of me. Brenda leaves Star house with intentions to never return.

Once Brenda left the house Victor got on his cell to contact Jay. He couldn't wait to tell him how Brenda thinks John is dead. "Yeah." Jay answered.

"I don't know what you did but it worked and she left. Oh and she thinks I did ya man. I just went along with it."

"Alright. One."

Victor felt like a burden had been lifted off his shoulders. That coked out bitch is gone! Jay is my family. I must groom him. He's definitely a warrior but he needs to be a businessman. Or else someone will rise up and seek his downfall.

Tiffany

June 1998

With Brenda out of the picture everything went back to business as usual, especially for Jay. Buffalo and I were still going strong living together but a part of me missed Mark. Mark satisfies the kid in me. I called him and we met up at McDonald's in the Gallery for old times. We just talked about how we used to be. That time he stole a car and we got arrested. I couldn't believe he was going to college. Playing basketball had landed him a full scholarship.He has a girlfriend, the white girl from his block. I don't even want to remember her name. Being with Buffalo is like being a working wife. I love him and he takes care of me even though I work. He allows me to keep my money. On the inside deep down I wonder what would have happened if I stayed with Mark? Mark had changed a lot; he seems more stable. He went to prom. I don't think I'll ever experience that. His uncle has a baby now. Maybe I should have ran away there instead...nope his uncle wouldn't have allowed that. When we parted ways we hugged and he kissed me on the lips. I still feel love between us but we weren't who we used to be.

I convinced Keke to visit Aunt Pat today. It wasn't easy because Keke really don't fuck with me since Tommy is gone. After the baby was born she went back to Hicks Street as a full blown whore. Keke fucks and sucks more than all the girls. During her pregnancy she wouldn't speak to me or Janell. She declined all our phone calls. Keke even had Dee send us away from the house. I approached her one night at Hicks Street, I put a gun to her head and told her to stop hiding from me. "You crazy bitch!" Keke yelled once I lowered the twenty two.

I had Rambo take us to Baltimore Avenue and we walked the rest of the way. Keke's son is so cute he resembles his grandfather. I wonder if Keke notices or acknowledges it. I'm glad he doesn't look like Tommy's disgusting ass. "We owe it to Aunt Pat that she sees we are alive. You have a child she should know."

"I'm only doing this since you threatened to kill me! My mother didn't care when she let my dad kill my first baby."

"That was messed up but he only wanted what was best for you! Look at me Keke! My dad is locked up for me!"

"Uh huh…"

"Don't you miss the twins?"

"Yeah. You got your brother Tiffany. You always have. When I saw that Little John was Jay I was too scared. I just pretended I never saw him. Or so I thought. He saw me...but he didn't say anything. They said he's the man, stay out the man way or get got. Now you say see my mom or get got. Y'all just some killers."

Tiffany never thought of it that way, but she wasn't going to dwell on the statement at that moment. Tiffany helped Keke with her stroller and then rang the doorbell. Aunt Pat answers the door to see her daughter holding a baby boy that looked like Jake. As soon as they entered the house Pat hugged Keke. Tiffany stood and watched the tears flow down her aunt's eyes. I knew this was the right thing to do. "Oh my God! I pray every night that y'all are safe! I'm so sorry about everything! Is this my grandchild?" Pat picks up the baby to stare in his eyes. "He looks just like your father!"

"I know. How are you? Where are the twins?" Keke asked as she got herself settled with the baby's things.

"I'm better now. The twins are out with Simone. Are y'all staying long? Tiffany I'm happy to see you too!"

"I know Aunt Pat."

"I have been writing to your dad. He said you have seen him, but you haven't written to him in a while?"

Tiffany sits on the couch. "No I have not. I have been working. Can you let him know I'm fine though please."

"I will. You work huh? Both of you look like a million bucks! I almost didn't recognize you two."

Pat goes into the kitchen to grab cans of Pepsi. Tiffany and Keke each take a can.

"We will stay a little Mom but then we have to get home. My son's name is Devin. That is what I was going to name my first baby if it was a boy."

"Come on Keke...you still went on and had another. I figured you would. You and Jake are very stubborn. Your brothers are doing great. Jason is boxing and JJ plays basketball!"

"That's great Mom. I will do my best to come visit more."

"I'm happy to hear. Well I'm off today so y'all picked the right time for a visit! I can cook us something. Fry up some fish or chicken. Tiffany, so how are you feeling about your house being on the news?"

"I'm okay Aunt Pat...nothing but bad memories. Whatever you decide to cook is fine with me, I'm hungry!" Keke gave Tiffany a dirty look as she made that statement.

"Great. I know that damn Brenda had something to do with it…you know she ran down south right?"

"Really with Mabel?"

"At first yeah…but then she ran off with some older man. Mabel hasn't seen her or heard from her."

Tiffany thinks to herself, ``Let her stay gone. If she comes back that murder weapon will fall into police hands. The best part about what we did is that she actually thinks my Dad is dead!

"Keke, are you living with Devin's father?"

"No…he's dead. I found out I was pregnant after his death." Keke looks at Tiffany. Tiffany ignores Keke's emotions.

"I'm sorry to hear. If y'all ever wanna come home…"

"Mom, let's just enjoy the visit okay?"

Pat stops yelling from the kitchen and strictly focuses on cooking. Tiffany cuts her eyes at Keke. "Your mom misses you clearly. Don't be so hard on her. We know we can't ever come back."

"Oh shut up! After dinner I wanna go home! I need to get ready for tonight. A new client coming in Dee said…with big money! I heard he's trying to do business with Jay too. Maybe this pussy will reel him in!"

Keke is such a whore, Tiffany concluded. Keke would rather go jump on some strange dick than be with her mother. Aunt Pat isn't perfect but I know she did do her best. Brenda never gave a damn about us. Tiffany takes Devin from Keke and starts rocking him up and down her knee. Devin smiles.

Tiffany was happy to sit at the table for old times sake and enjoy a dinner made by Aunt Pat. She could tell Aunt Pat had a lot she wanted to say or ask but knew it was best to not dwell. Tiffany ate every bit of the food that was prepared. Fried fish, mash potatoes, corn, and biscuits. She did miss her Aunt's cooking. Keke did too even though she tried to play it cool. Pat ate and helped her grandson happily. He occasionally grabbed his grandmother's fork.

That Night

Hicks Street is really jumping tonight. All these new players are here spending mad money! They ain't even asking for sex! Just lap dances and a few hand jobs. They looked good too! A mixture of Black dudes and Hispanics just throwing money everywhere. Buffalo and Tory looked extremely pleased with the turnout. I was trying to figure out who was the 'man in charge' of the crew, but Keke spotted him before I could. He was tall, brown skin with a beard, fresh waves, and muscular. Damn he's fine! He looks better than Buffalo. Keke was going hard on his lap too. I couldn't be mad at her. Tara comes up and slaps Tiffany on the butt. "Hey baby girl!" Tara greets Tiffany and continues to walk by with two regulars behind her. Tara is so beautiful. Janell notices Tiffany daydreaming, she walks up to her. "Earth to Tiffany!" Janell yells.

"Don't start Janell. You see Keke on that fine ass dude?" Janell looks over.

"Damn bitch! Aye this is one helluva night! I don't even know where to put all this money! Can we go shopping tomorrow?"

"Yeah we can do that." Tiffany kept her eye on Keke; she noticed Keke was taking his number. I may have to put Jay on this. As far as I know no deals have been made this guy is fine but he ain't in the family yet. Keke is being too friendly. Tiffany walks over to Buffalo. Buffalo was entertaining a couple of the new guys. "Yo, can I speak with you for a minute?"

Buffalo takes a shot of Hennessy before answering. " Yup. Give me a minute y'all."

Buffalo and Tiffany go upstairs to the dressing room. He thought she wanted a quickie and he started grabbing on her thong. "Boy stop! I don't want any, not right now!"

"Oh! Well what do you take me away from work for?"

"Who is the guy Keke is pushing up on hard?"

"Max. He's the boss. Why?"

"Just checking. Is he good with Jay?"

"Jay ain't met him yet. You know this is Tory's guy. He met me in Jersey awhile back."

"Okay. That's all...bye!" Tiffany grabs Buffalo's jean imprint of where his penis is.

"Really!" Buffalo walks out the room hard and disappointed.

When Tiffany arrived back down to the party she saw that Keke had not left Max's side.

Tiffany's Sixteenth Birthday

1998

If it wasn't for Buffalo I wouldn't have cared about today being my birthday. I just decided to let that part of my life go as far as celebrating important dates just in case enemies were watching. When I woke up this morning I could smell pancakes being made. When I came downstairs the living room and dining room had balloons everywhere. Breakfast was on the table with Buffalo, Tory, Mike, and Janell waiting for me to join them. "All this for me?" Tiffany asked, staring at the pancakes, cheese grits, eggs, and turkey bacon. "Yeah now come on we are hungry!" Janell responds by reaching for the pancakes. Everyone was sitting at the table content with the food and each other. I really appreciate Tyreek for this. For his birthday I just buy him clothes or sneakers. He really treats me well. I truly can't complain about that.

"I told Jay about breakfast. He said he would see you later and he had business to get to." Buffalo explains to Tiffany stroking her hand.

"What's happening later? I don't want a party." Tiffany shakes her head.

"Well Jay is giving you one!" Mike blurs out. Janell punches Mike in the arm.

"You got a big ass mouth! It's supposed to be a surprise!"

"It doesn't feel the same without my dad." Tiffany was about to get up from the table but Buffalo stopped her.

"Speaking of your Pops...look he sent this card to the P.O. Box we set up."

Tiffany's face lights up with joy. Yes! He rips it open. John hand made his daughter a beautiful birthday card: *Happy Birthday to my beautiful, wonderful, loving daughter. I think of you everyday! I love you always...Please enjoy this day!*

Tears flow down Tiffany's eyes. Okay Tiffany get it together. So Jay is giving me a party. I'm going to enjoy it damn it! "Aight y'all we are partying tonight!"

Tory's cell phone rings. "It's Jay."

"Yo!" Tory answers.

"Get to the spot." Jay demands and then hangs up.

"I gotta meet Jay. He doesn't sound happy either. Fuck!"

"Calm down, it might not be about nothing." Mike assures.

Jay

Tiffany's Sixteenth Birthday

Jay sat at his desk waiting patiently for Tory to arrive. Hazel sat at the opposite side of the desk. "Do you think he knows?" Hazel asked Jay as she counted her money. Jay looks at the money and then he looks at the bag he placed on the desk.

"It doesn't matter at this point."

As Jay was speaking Rambo escorted Tory into the office. Hazel got up from her chair and pointed for Tory to sit down. She took out her thirty eight. Tory immediately got nervous. "Aye, Jay what's going on?"

"You tell me Tory? Open the bag!"

Tory opens the bag to a hand. He gets up from the table. Hazel grabs him and makes Tory sit back down.

"You biting the hand that feeds you Tory? With these piece of shit Jersey niggas?"

"Naw! I swear!! When you said no to Max I honored that! I don't know anything about this shit! I swear I swear!"

"What do you think Hazel?"

"I think somebody didn't like being told no."

Tory starts pleading for his life to Jay. "Don't kill me! I'm loyal. I don't know what the fuck is going on!"

"Shut yo pathetic ass up! Tell everybody to be strapped! We are at war! We are still having Tiffany's party, we just will double up on security!"

Tory leaves the office thankful to be still alive.

"Max thinks he's gonna move me out huh? Well…"

"I'm gonna send word out. Which car are we taking to New York?"

"Get a new one. I'm not taking any chances. For Max to know where one of the stash houses is definitely an inside job."

Hazel leaves out. Jay gets on the cell to call Victor. He lets him know to be prepared for war.

Tiffany's Party New York City

Tiffany's Sixteenth Birthday

Tiffany was so excited that she was celebrating her birthday in New York at a club owned by Victor. Victor was instructed by Jay not to invite Star in case she would recognize him or Tiffany. Buffalo brought Tiffany a sexy red party dress with diamond hoop earrings. Janell was more excited than Tiffany. She was in the car window amazed by the tall buildings and bright lights. Like a big kid she pointed at everything she had never seen before. Janell wore a sparkle spaghetti strap party dress with diamond studs. Recently Janell was adventurous and got her first tattoo, a pair of lips on her left breast. Tiffany got her belly button pierced. She wasn't sure about tattoos just yet. The trip to New York involved five cars. One of the cars Keke was in accompanied by Rambo. Rambo has a huge crush on Keke but she wouldn't give him the time of day. Hazel had to stay in Philly in case anything popped off while they celebrated Tiffany's big night.

Victor's club was huge with three floors. The third floor is where Tiffany's party was being held. Big bright neon lights flashed everywhere, sexy people on the dance floor, and the DJ kept them moving. Only big time players were invited personally by Jay. Jay has made many connections with New York and North Jersey. All of the crew came and blessed Tiffany with money, jewelry, and bottles of champagne. Buffalo at first was getting a little jealous from all the attention Tiffany was getting. He quickly got it together when Jay came by with a big bottle of Hennessy. "Yo! Sis you fuckin' with ya party?"

"Hell yeah!" Tiffany gets up to give Jay a hug. Janell comes back from off the dance floor with Mike. "Girl when are you gonna get on this floor with me?" Janell yells to Tiffany. Tiffany gets up from her V.I.P. Section to join her best friend on the dance floor. She sees Keke out the corner of her eye staring down at her phone. I guess Keke ain't in the mood as usual. Tiffany and Janell dance hard on the floor shaking and bending their backbones all the way down to the floor. Their dancing was so sexy it caught the attention of Tara. She walks over to Tiffany, takes her hand, and starts dancing with her. Janell goes to the opposite side putting Tiffany in the middle. By now all the men come out and watch the three girls as if they were hypnotized.

In the midst of the sexy dancing gunshots break out. The club goes crazy, people begin running and stepping on each other. Tiffany, Janell, and Tara are rushed out by Rambo. Tiffany sees Jay walking the opposite way. "No!!! What the fuck is Jay doing?" Tiffany tried to break free from Rambo. She bit him and ran towards her brother. "Look Janell and Tara let's go!!! Now!!!" Janell and Tara did as they were told. Tiffany followed Jay's voice. "Come out bitch!" Jay yells as he makes a warning shot. The hallway was kind of dark. Tiffany noticed a shadow in the corner the opposite of Jay. She runs behind her brother. "Jay..."

Jay is not pleased to see Tiffany but he sees her signaling him to the shadow. He nods. Tiffany grabs Jay's glock from the back of his jeans. The shadow begins to crawl leaving a blood trail. Tiffany lighty runs up to figure and kicks him down. She points the gun to his head. The lights come back on. Tiffany recognizes the guy from Hicks Street house. "The fuck is going on?" Tiffany asked Jay.

"It's Max, he didn't like being told no! Now he thinks he's gonna punk me out my shit!"

Tiffany without hesitation finishes the job her brother started, she unloads three shots to the tattooed bald

Hispanic head. On my birthday though? What a way to remember turning sixteen! Tiffany and Jay hear Victor yelling for them. He runs down the hall to meet them. "Come on, it's a secret way out!" Victor takes Tiffany and Jay to safety. "What about the cops?" Tiffany asked Victor.

"I got cops, don't worry about nothing...you family."

"Jay, how many of Max's men were there?"

"It looks like he just sent that one. He got Tory. I believe that's all he was after tonight. Once I saw Tory down I shot back and followed him."

"Why did you still have this damn party? I mean a new car would've been nice!"

"Ain't nobody gonna stop me from doin' shit! You understand we killin' all them mothafuckas!!!"

Victor gives Jay one of his cars to drive back to Philly in. On the road Tiffany called Janell to let her know everything was okay. By this time everyone else was either back in Philly or halfway there. During a war all of Jay's soldiers know to go to the safe in West Philly and wait for his arrival. Tiffany's mind is racing during the drive. Tory's dead! How did they know where we would be? Oh no she wouldn't! Would she? Tiffany thinks about how Keke was acting tonight. Keke was very distant and constantly checking her phone. I did see her and Max exchange cell numbers. "Jay when the shooting started, where was Keke?"

"Keke wasn't around. I think she got up to go to the bar or something. Why?"

"She was awfully cozy with Max that night at Hicks Street."

Jay's cell phone goes off its Hazel.

"Yo!"

"Hicks Street has been hit."

"What?"

"Shit is shut down! Cops raided it. Dee is locked up!"

Jay hangs up the phone. "Cops raided Hicks Street! Fuck!!"

"Yo pay attention to the road! Don't draw any attention on this highway. We are almost there."

The rest of the ride was dead silent. Tiffany could only imagine what was on her brother's mind. Keke is fuckin' dead! I don't care if she's my cousin! That bitch didn't even want to see her own mother. Tiffany watched Jay's facial expressions, he looked super pissed. Don't say anything, just wait until we get to the safe house. Jay parked the car a block away from the safe house, he and Tiffany entered the house through the back way. All his soldiers took up the entire downstairs including Mike and Buffalo who just lost their brother. Tiffany ran and hugged Buffalo but he wasn't hugging her back. Janell heard Tiffany's voice from upstairs and came down immediately. Hazel entered the house shortly after. Jay stood in the middle of the living room. "Aight we gotta move to plan B. Hicks Street is dead! In the morning Rambo's Auntie is gonna bail Dee out of jail. All the girls were moved…who did Keke ride with back?"

"Keke disappeared. She wasn't with the girls at the club and I didn't see her get in the other cars." Rambo answered.

"We were played by a bitch that's why Max made his bitch ass moves.Bring Keke back to me alive! I'm personally gonna take care of that bitch" Jay announced.

All the soldiers left the safe house except Mike and Buffalo, Jay ordered them to stay.

"Max is dead! Keke is dead! You know it's her revenge for her old boy. I thought about killing her after we did him. I thought she would get over it after the baby was born. You can't go home. I'm putting y'all in one of my apartments up the street."

Buffalo and Mike just stayed silent while Jay talked. Tiffany and Janell sat at the dining room table. "Fuckin' Keke that bitch ain't been right." Janell expresses her anger to Tiffany while lighting a black and mild. "You know I know...but they ain't gonna find Keke here. If they didn't see her in the crowd it's because she was already picked up."

Tiffany turns to Jay. "Yo! Jay we gotta call Victor...get him to run the tapes that's how we gonna find Keke." Jay took his sister's orders and called Victor. "Aye can you run them tapes back? Can't find Keke."

"Okay. Give me two hours" Victor says

"We will find out in two hours."

"I told Tory not to fuck with them. I told him that the bull seemed grimy." Buffalo cries. Mike stayed quiet.

"Family can sometimes be your worst enemy." Jay states.

Two Hours Later...

Victor called Jay two hours later as he said he would. By this time Jay is at the garage going over plans to hit Max directly with Tiffany and Hazel. He sent Buffalo and Mike to their house in South Philly in case someone was there waiting to strike. So far that wasn't the case. Jay felt that the move for tonight was strictly to kill Tory. Hearing back from Victor on time was a plus. "I found your girl. She was picked up by a Cadillac with Jersey plates. She walked herself out of the club after she received a call. Moments later the shooting begins. She was definitely in on it."

"Aight. One."

"What did he say?" Hazel asked.

"Keke was part of the set up. Tiff you was right she ain't here in Philly. She got picked up by a car from Jersey."

"Told you. She's stupid but not that stupid. So we gotta go to them!"

"I put my man on them awhile back when they first started coming around. I know where a few stash houses are. Keke could be in one of them."

"Where is Devin?" Hazel asked.

"With his grandma…I should've known something was up when she said that my Aunt was gonna watch him" Tiffany answers Hazel while realizing how Keke really went about setting them up.

The Hunt for Keke

It's been two weeks since our operation was compromised by Keke and Max. We have eyes all over Jersey and Philly. There was one more shoot out since that night. Four of Max's men showed up to our house in South Philly. Jay put Mike, Rambo, and a few others in that house to watch over. We only lost one that night but that was his fault. Some dude named Joe insisted that he knew how to use some heavy ass gun. Anyway he shot himself! Mike reported back to Jay that all them niggas was dead. Jay wanted all Max's men cut up and delivered to Jersey. Hazel was on the delivery part. Buffalo and were in charge of looking for Keke. On a stakeout we saw one of Max's men take the package into one of stash houses. We could hear them yelling and cussing. In these past two weeks we saw the black Cadillac Keke got in but no Keke. We haven't spotted Max either. The fuck they go on vacation?

Business went back on track once plan B took full effect, Jay wasn't having it no other way. Dee is locked up so now Mike has to be in charge of the girls. The new house was in Southwest on Regent Street. Jay has it set up as an invite only until Max's head is in his possession. I have barely slept since that night. When I do, my semi automatic pistol is right next to me. I have never been in no shit like this before! Jay is like a kid in the candy store. He loves this street shit. Did we watch too many movies growing up? I mean he's reckless. We had to talk him out of setting our old trap house on fire. Jay believes in no evidence and no witnesses. I asked Hazel to drive me by Aunt Pat's house to see if Keke would come there for Devin. I saw the twins and Devin go with Aunt Sarah. They are getting so big. I wish I could greet them. Now I know how Jay must have felt seeing me and not being able to interact with me. Once they drove off I put my cell number in the mailbox. I know I will check the mail before she goes out to work. "Let's be out Hazel."

During the ride back to the garage Hazel started asking Tiffany questions that she's been holding back from asking Jay.

"Tiffany you're sixteen right?"

"Yeah."

"Jay the oldest right? So he's like eighteen or nineteen?"

I couldn't tell her that the man she's head over heels for is only fourteen! I know she would understand how young he is if she didn't have feelings for him. Jay took over and grown men followed him. I know she's asking because she keeps trying to push Jay to have sex. I told him to do it. I mean he's a boy. It's different for boys and older women.

"Yeah Hazel. What's on your mind?"

"He won't sleep with me. I mean I don't know what to do! Is it another bitch? You would tell me right Tiffany? I'll kill her if it is."

"Hazel, when do you think Jay got time for another bitch? Give him time."

We stopped at the McDonald's drive thru and it brought back memories of Mark. Shit as of right now chasing him around would be a lot less stressful than making sure I don't get shot or killed. Buffalo was at the garage with Jay giving him a report on the current status of Max and Keke.

"So I saw Max go to his stash house in Camden no Keke though. He looks like he is feeling this heat. I know he is Jay."

"Tiffany, you went to her mom's house?"

"Yeah her son is still there no sign of her. I left my number."

"Smart. You're gonna need another phone though because when she calls you gotta toss it. Hazel, go get her another phone from my man."

Hazel left out to do as she was told.

"Max is in Jersey for now. I think one of the niggas y'all took out was his brother. We're gonna be seeing Max real soon. You're right Buff, he's definitely feeling that shit now."

August 1, 1998

Today felt almost like a normal day. There haven't been any more shootouts. All the local independents were too scared to try anything once word got out about us moving out on Max. Especially the ones who had New Jersey connections they voluntarily switched to us. This made Victor very happy and very rich. I still haven't heard anything from Aunt Pat though. Last time I went over to check for Keke it was still the same routine. The twins and Devin were leaving with Aunt Sarah. Buffalo has been distant towards me. We stay in the apartment together, however we don't sleep together. We haven't had sex since my birthday. I don't know what to do. I try to still show him love but he doesn't seem to care. Mike said he could be depressed about Tory. Janell is coming over to help me take my mind off Buffalo's depression. Mike is handling Tory's death just fine. Buffalo probably blames himself or something.

Janell and Tiffany sit in the living room watching movies. They got pizza, soda, and chocolate chip cookies. They decided to watch Bad Boys for laughs and action. Tiffany's old cell phone was ringing, she thought it was Aunt Pat.

"Hey Mark!"

Janell looked up from the sofa when she heard Mark's name.

"Hey Tiffany. I'm leaving for college in a couple weeks. I wanna see you before I leave please."

"Okay…when?"

"Today."

"I'll see what I can do."

"Please Tiffany."

"Okay…I will come to you. Give me like a few hours."

Tiffany gets off the phone with Mark. Janell is in her face. "Mark?"

"Yeah…we stayed friends. He leaves for college in a couple of weeks and he wants to hang out."

"What about your man?"

"He's not thinking about me!" Tiffany kisses Janell on the forehead and gets up from the couch. "Gay ass!" Janell yells.

"You are too!"

"Not as gay as you!"

Tiffany got in the shower. Everything that is going on right now seeing Mark will make me happy. I deserve to be happy right now. My birthday was ruined by Keke. People want to kill me and my family over drug territories! At least with Mark I can just be Tiffany. Tiffany made a mental note to still carry her strap. When Tiffany got back from showering and getting dressed Janell was laying on the couch naked. "Janell what are you doing?"

"Why are you going to see Mark? Stay here with me! I thought we were finally gonna you know...since Buffalo ain't giving you none."

"I'm going to see Mark, Janell. I'm not exactly ready for that yet. Clearly you are though!" Tiffany stares at her best friend's body. She is so beautiful but no, not yet. As much as I would love to explore being with a girl. I still want men. "Janell please get dressed!"

Janell's face was full of disappointment. She was ready to give herself to Tiffany. "Okay, go see stupid Mark. You want me to be here when you get back?"

"No. I don't want to put you in a position to lie for me if Buffalo gets home before me."

Janell got dressed and they both left the house together. Tiffany drove to Mark's house with so many different emotions going through her. I'm so happy for Mark. I'm glad he wants to see me before leaving for college. Why did things end that way between us? But you already know your life has to change. You're not even a real teenager…you carry guns now…you've killed two people! Mark would never understand my life if I told him the full truth. Would he look at me the same? I don't even look at me the same. I'm looking for my own cousin to kill her! Keke is a bitch and been a bitch! She treated her parents horribly! If Daddy didn't figure it out for himself about Uncle Todd I would still be a victim. Brenda would still be making our lives hell. Grandma Mabel would still be rocking her fat ass in the damn chair! We would still be sharing one bed! I wouldn't be rich! I never want to go back to that life.

Mark was standing in the doorway waiting for Tiffany. Tiffany quickly parked her car to greet him. Her stomach was filled with butterflies. She ran up and hugged him tight. Tiffany immediately started crying on Mark's shoulder. He looked down at her confused. "Tiffany, I will come back for the holidays."

"Shut up! I didn't mean to start crying like that… I have a lot going on."

"I see you drive! You're wearing diamonds. Come in and catch me up."

Nobody was home which was the norm for Mark. They sat on the couch in the living room that we were caught having sex on. "Everything is fucked up at the moment but it's okay."

"What happened Tiffany?"

"I wanna tell you but I don't want you to look at me differently."

"Look at you differently? You have changed appearance wise but you're still Tiffany. I know I have changed. I was with a white girl."

Tiffany started laughing. "Was?"

"We broke up. I'm cool though. College is gonna have more women. They won't be you though Tiffany."

Tiffany looks at Mark and she begins to feel like that little girl in Children's Hospital with a crush. "Is that why I'm here?"

"No. I miss you...I wanted to see you before I start college. I wasn't making it up."

"What do you wanna do?"

"First. I need you to tell me who's buying you all the diamonds? What's up with the car? Your family? Who are you now Tiffany?"

Tiffany takes a deep breath. "Mark...I'm a stripper, well there's a war right now I have been on lookout...I..." Tiffany starts crying.

"Shh...it's okay. I'm glad you're alive. A war?"

"Yeah…Keke's stupid ass…look at the end of it I'm never going back to my old life."

Tiffany shows Mark her gun. He is startled at first but calms down. Mark takes the gun from Tiffany and places it on the coffee table. Mark looks at Tiffany in the eyes. "It doesn't matter what is going on. I don't care what you have done." Mark starts kissing Tiffany passionately. Tiffany kisses Mark with the same passion plus more without thinking she started taking off his shirt. Mark stops Tiffany to take her upstairs to his room. Mark laid Tiffany down on his bed and made her forget about everything.

Two Hours Later...

Tiffany's phones have been going off back to back for the last hour. She put them on silent prior to seeing Mark. Tiffany checks her phones to see that Aunt Pat, Hazel, Jay, Buffalo, and Janell had called. Oh shit! She looks over at Mark who is asleep. Tiffany chooses not to disturb him so she grabs her clothes and quickly gets dressed. Before she leaves she kisses him on the head. Tiffany hurry's to grab her gun off the table to leave out of Mark's house. Once she got in her car she decided to call Janell first. "Yo! Bitch!!! What the fuck were you doing? We need you at the spot now!" Janell yells at Tiffany. Tiffany can tell that it's urgent. I really got caught up in my feelings. Shit! Now something done popped off. Mark I know you were only trying to help, I should've been more mindful. I'm in a war! Stupid Tiffany! Stop letting your emotions get the best of you.

When Tiffany arrived at the safe house Jay was furious. He was pacing back and forth in the living room holding his gun. Hazel was sitting at the table with the soldiers in silence blasting DMX. Janell, Mike, and Buffalo sat in the living room watching Jay. "Where the fuck were you Tiffany huh?" Jay demands.

"I took a drive, Jay. What's going on?"

"What's going on? Ha! Tiffany wants to know what's going on?!? We are at war! Shit is always gonna pop off until the target is dead! You remember that don't you?"

"Yeah Jay."

"Keke is dead! They put her body in a trash bag in front of her mom's door!"

Tiffany looked at her phone to see that Aunt Pat left her a voicemail. She played it, all she could hear was Aunt Pat screaming and crying that her daughter was gone. To think we were gonna kill her. "She doesn't know anything about Jay. I'm gonna get rid of this burner."

"Now Tiffany! Go smash that shit up! We don't need no police on us."

Tiffany goes into the kitchen and finds a hammer to smash the cellphone with.

"You're gonna have to go see her. See what she told the cops."

"Was her body chopped up?"

"No, she was stabbed multiple times and beaten up. Max waited on purpose for this shit. This is very personal to him so I know we can get him. Go take care of that part first. I got a plan Tiff. He hasn't move on nobody out here or the niggas out of town he wants me."

Tiffany looks at Buffalo and she can tell he wants to talk to her about where she's been, he knows now isn't the time. Tiffany sits next to Janell on the couch instead. "Do you have anyone looking out to let me know when I can go there?"

"Yeah once he hits me up…you are up."

Waiting for the signal to go to Aunt Pat's house was killing Tiffany inside. Figuring out what to say without incriminating myself is what she needs to figure out. Buffalo walks up to Tiffany. "Can we talk in private upstairs?" Tiffany shakes her head yes. Might as well see what he has to say. Everything else is going to shit. Tiffany and Buffalo go upstairs to one of the bedrooms. "Where were you really Tiffany?"

"I went for a drive… I needed to clear my head. You have been distant and it's just so much going on."

Buffalo looked at Tiffany and figured it was best to not pry her with questions. "Okay. We can't afford anymore slip ups Tiff. I love you."

"I love you too." Buffalo walks out of the room. Tiffany sits down on the bed. She checks her phone and realizes that she never gave Mark her new number. She calls him immediately but hangs up.

Aunt Pat House

Tiffany planned out how she was gonna play it with Aunt Pat. Before she rang the doorbell Tiffany was crying hysterically. Aunt Sarah answers the door with anguish in her eyes. She can barely hug Tiffany. The twins sat in the living room on the floor with their nephew. Devin stayed content laying on his Elmo blanket kicking his feet. When JJ noticed Tiffany he got up and hugged her so tight. "Tiffany! I miss you so much!"

"I missed you too! You're so big! Hey Jason!"

Jason just looked and turned his head up. Tiffany could tell Jason had been crying.

Aunt Pat was sitting in the dining room smoking a cigarette with a bottle of Jack Daniels to the left of her.

"Tiffany I called you! Your phone goes straight to voicemail!"

"I lost it...when you called me I was so upset...what happened?"

"I came out to check the mail and I saw..." Pat starts crying. Tiffany consoles her aunt.

"I thought everything was ok with Keke, she seemed happy about a new boyfriend."

"New boyfriend...right...that's what she told me...she said she was going away and now she's dead! Have you ever seen her boyfriend Tiffany? He probably did this to my baby!" Pat takes a long drag of her cigarette. I see time has turned my Aunt Pat into Brenda, smoking cigarettes and drinking straight out the bottle. Her joyful face is now filled with pain. Keke put this on herself. All of it. We were just gonna shoot her. Make it look like she ran off. Max tortured Keke. I never wanted Aunt Pat to feel like this.

"To see my daughter in a trash bag like she's nothing." Pat starts crying again and fills Tiffany's shoulders with her tears.

"The police are gonna find out who did this, Aunt Pat."

"Probably not. No suspects...I have to go properly identify her body tomorrow...Keke just changed."

"I know she and I hadn't been close in a long time."

"She called me and was extremely happy. She asked me to watch the baby. I said sure, she came over with Devin. She didn't tell me her boyfriend's name. I didn't want to press her ya know? I was just glad to see her. The cops asked me if she was on drugs!" Pat shakes her head. "I told them I don't know! They ask was she a gang affiliate? Keke in a gang? I just feel like she got mixed up in the wrong crowd. I don't know anything about either of you! Over the phone I did ask Keke where you were. She said y'all don't live together and I could tell that made her upset…she always was jealous of our relationship."

Tiffany remained quiet. The police aren't going to dig too deep into this. Just another black girl runaway. "Have you called Grandma Mabel?"

"I did, she's gonna come up for the funeral but that's about it." Pat cries and smokes. Aunt Sarah comes to the table. "Who are you running around with? Huh? Dressed like that? You keep it up, you're gonna end up like Keke!"

Tiffany made a conscious decision to get up from the table. Don't argue with her. "Are you leaving Tiffany?" Aunt Pat asked with her eyes filled with tears.

"I'll be back, Aunt Pat."

"No she won't! You keep whatever it is you got going on little girl away from this house! Do you hear me? Don't come back here!" Aunt Sarah screams to Tiffany.

"Aunt Sarah! Tiffany doesn't have anything to do with it! Tiffany, please don't leave!" Aunt Pat pleads to Tiffany. Tiffany didn't say a word when she left her Aunt's house and shut the door never to return.

The War Ends

After I saw Aunt Pat that night I reported back to Jay everything that happened. He almost reminded me of Little John when I expressed to him the pain Aunt Pat was in. I could see he had a little remorse in him. To compensate for Aunt Pat's loss Jay told Hazel to put money in the mailbox to pay for Keke's funeral. No doubt Keke was a jealous, twisted, ungrateful bitch who may have gotten what she deserved. Aunt Pat was our concern. We put eyes on Keke's funeral. It was reported to be small at a funeral home in West Philly. Keke's funeral was closed casket. The twins cried non stop. Devin he's a baby so he will never have to remember this day. A part of me wanted to be there for Aunt Pat, I mean all the times she's been there for me. I don't need any shit from Aunt Sarah. She probably thinks I'm responsible somehow.

I made sure I called Mark with my new number. I don't want him to think I abandoned him. He told me he loves me and wants me to come out to his college for visits. Mark asked me for another chance. I asked him if we could take things slow. Buffalo has started almost acting like himself. We are still in war mode but he's opening up again to me. We finally had sex. I felt kind of bad for cheating on him with Mark. At the same time I needed Mark. Buffalo wasn't as good as Mark when we did it. It's like the passion is gone. Then I started wondering if he could tell I was with someone else but I don't think so.

Jay's big plan to end the war with Max is to go down tonight. We are taking a big risk with this plan truthfully. We won't be in our territory. Victor promised to get out of town back up so that puts me at ease. I have been practicing all week with Hazel how to properly shoot a gun. For this type of life being able to kill at a distance is your best bet. Hazel reminds me of the chick from 'The Long Kiss Goodnight' she could shoot from anywhere. I have been watching the movie every night since practicing with her. She told me she's known how to use a gun since the age of nine. She was born into a gang called Rojo Death. Her whole family was in it! I could tell Hazel has been exposed to more violence and drug life than I could ever imagine. I thought we had it rough growing up with Brenda. Hazel has lived in war her entire life. Jay at first didn't want me on the plan but anything goes at this point. Max dumped Keke on Aunt Pat's door like trash and then he did a 'Jay' move. He burnt down our stash house in North Jersey. Jay lost four soldiers that day and a lot of money. One of the soldiers was Jerry's cousin. Jay promised Jerry revenge with Max's head on a platter. Jerry said Daddy has been teaching him how to read better. To know my Daddy is okay always makes me feel better. So for this war I'm going all out. I will have my brothers back just like I know he will have mine.

Before the war I had to see Janell. She had been blowing up my cell phone all day. Janell is strictly in the dance world. She came out and watched Hazel shoot rounds one day. We gave her a twenty two to try out. We told her to shoot at the cans. She shot one can down and dropped the gun. I won't force her to be anything else but what she is. I accept that she's strictly a dancer, fighter, and of course my best friend. It was best to stay low while with Janell today. We hung out at the apartment watching cartoons. I didn't want to think about tonight. "Tiffany, are you scared?" Janell asked.

"I don't know... I know I'm coming back alive." Tiffany kisses Janell on her forehead.

"I'm scared for you Tiffany... I don't know what I would do without you. Where's Buffalo?"

"He's at the stash house with Jay. I'm gonna meet them there. Hazel is picking me up."

"Tiffany, do you ever wish we just stayed home that day at your Aunt house? Instead of me taking you to see Mike?"

"No. I wouldn't have my brother or better contact with my father. It seems fucked up but it's best this way."

"I thought about it. But I guess I never thought about it from your point of view. Please come back to me, Tiffany." Janell lays on Tiffany's lap.

"I am, don't you worry about that."

That Night

The War Ends

Hazel came to pick up Tiffany right on schedule. Tiffany dressed as light as possible like Hazel instructed her. Black tights, white tank top, and Nike sneakers. She put her weave up in a high bun. Tiffany carries her gun but she knows Jay will be providing her with another. Tiffany allowed Janell to stay at the apartment to feel safe. Hazel and Tiffany rode in silence to Jay's stash house in North Philly.

Jay, Mike, Buffalo, Rambo, and all of Jay's soldiers were loading up all their guns. Jay tosses me a revolver. Hazel goes upstairs to change. When she came back down Jay went over the plans again.

"Alright so word is this nigga Max been staying at one of my man's hotels out Jersey. We're gonna get him in the parking garage. Everything is tight in Jersey. He's supposed to be going to a party in like two hours. Let's go get this bitch!"

Victor's brother owns the little high end hotel in Jersey. The security is in on the whole operation and prepared for a blood bath. We know that Max is three trucks deep at the hotel. Victor promised us the getaway cars after this deed is done. Victor's brother on purpose did not take on any new guest other than the regular cheating husbands or players from Jersey. Max has no idea he's going to die tonight.

I rode in the car with Jay, Hazel, Mike, and Buffalo. Buffalo kept rubbing Tiffany's leg and smiling at her. "When this is over I want to give it to you properly. I know I haven't been myself." Tiffany smiles at Buffalo.

When we got to the garage Jay called Victor as planned. The parking garage has only a car entrance and two exit levels with stairs. We parked all our cars on the opposite side of Max's three trucks. As planned we stayed low in the cars with the lights out. The security in the garage dimmed the lights. Max and his crew came off the elevators about fifteen guys deep. The lights in the garage go out as planned. We all get out of our cars. "What the fuck!" One of Max's soldiers yelled. The lights come back on. We immediately started shooting. Max and his crew shoot back. Hazel shot one of Max's soldiers in the head while he reached to get in the truck. I shot the biggest one in the shoulder, he fell back into the wall and then I followed up with a headshot from about three feet away like Hazel taught me. In the midst of all the shooting Rambo is dragging one of the soldiers to the car for safety. I couldn't make out who he was dragging since the lights were still dim, but I covered him for safety. I bust my guns at four of Max's soldiers. I was grazed in the right shoulder. I didn't care, I just kept shooting. "Tiff take cover!" Mike yells while shooting a guy from behind me. I looked around for a quick second and we appeared to be winning. Jay saw Max go through one of the stair exits he follows him. I crawled to the exit that I saw them run through. Max and Jay are fist fighting at the top of the garage. Both of their guns are empty and on the ground. Max punches Jay twice in the face. "You're just a punk kid playing in a grown man's game! Keke told me everything while I tortured her for days! She actually thought I loved her disloyal ass!" Jay spits the blood out his mouth and swings back at Max punching in the temple. Even though Max was at least twenty two years old and Jay fourteen they were built about the same in the body. Max stumbles to the ground. Jay kicks Max in the face several times. Tiffany stays to the side with her gun positioned to shoot Max if she had to. From the way Jay was kicking Max, Max appeared unconscious and his face full of blood. Jay reaches in his pocket for his knife. He grabs Max's head and cuts his throat. Tiffany walks up to her brother. "You want me to shoot him?" Tiffany asked.

"Naw he's dead." Jay and Tiffany watch Max's blood spill out his throat. Hazel comes up to hand Jay the machete to cut off Max's head as promised. Hazel threw his head in the black duffel bag. Victor and his security team arrived to check that the garage was clear from Max's men. "They're all dead Jay. Nobody is gonna fuck with you...your untouchable and you owe me fifty grand to clean all this shit up!" Victor and Jay laughed hard for about thirty seconds.

Back on the ground level there were bodies everywhere. Most of them belonged to Max's crew. Rambo came from out of the corner he took cover in with the body he dragged. "Yo um I don't know how to say this but ya boy is gone." Rambo stated.

"What boy?" Jay asked.

"Her boy...Mike's brother."

Tiffany and Mike ran over to the corner to see Buffalo dead. He had been shot in the chest. "Fuck!" Mike yelled. Tiffany just stares at his dead body. Tears began to flow down her eyes. Mike just kept screaming. "We can't take his body back!" Jay informed Mike. "Fuck! I know...I know..." Mike looks down at his brother for the last time. Tiffany kisses Buffalo's head. "A part of me will always love you." Tiffany whispers.

Everyone who made it alive got in the cars Victor provided to return back to Philly. Jay put Max's head in the trunk. Jay was extremely proud of taking down Max.

"Soon I'll be the king of them all...they're gonna tell stories about me...us!" Jay yells as Rambo drives out the parking garage.

When I came into the apartment Janell was laying on the couch sleeping. She probably was losing her mind waiting for me to come home. I don't know how to feel right now. I wanted to scream, cry, and throw shit around. However another part of me deep down feels like it's best this way. Buffalo changed once Tory died. He hadn't been on his game for him to be in this shit way longer than me or Jay. Buffalo's was too emotional. I mean I'm a girl, it's who we are. Buffalo was willing to ruin his deal with Jay just because he thought we were fucking. Maybe he wanted death.I was thankful that it was not me.

Tiffany takes off her clothes to get in the shower. All she could see is the faces of Todd, Keke, and Buffalo. Check your emotions Tiffany. Don't look for reasons to cry. Tiffany gets out of the shower to see Janell standing by the bathroom door. "Oh my God!!! Tiffany I was worried sick!"

"I'm here...Buffalo didn't make it."

"Tiffany I'm sorry..."

"Don't Janell. Let it be. Come on, let's go to the bedroom and get some sleep."

Tiffany

October 1998

"Tiffany Brown." The nurse yells into the waiting area at the free clinic. Tiffany gets up and follows the nurse to the exam room. "Take this cup to urinate in. Here's some wipes." The nurse hands Tiffany the cup and wipes. Tiffany goes to the bathroom quickly. She hands the nurse the cup. "Put on this gown so the doctor can examine you."

Tiffany looks at the nurse. "I just need you to check my pee."

"Young lady, this is part of the visit. Now get changed, the doctor will be with you shortly." Tiffany takes the gown.

Fuck what did I get myself into? I know it's stress. I have been on street duty since the Max war. I didn't want to think about Buffalo dying. So I run the stash house in West Philly and I'm a major hitter. Stop tripping bitch...you ain't pregnant. Just change your clothes, let them check you so you can be on your way. Tiffany changes into the gown. She just stares at all the pictures on the wall about teen pregnancy and HIV. I should get checked for that too. The doctor comes into the room. A black woman for a doctor is going to be interesting. She should be able to understand me. "Ms. Tiffany Brown, correct?"

"Yes."

"You haven't had your cycle since July correct?"

"Yeah…I know it's stress right?"

"No. You're pregnant. I need to examine you, please lay back, and place your feet on the stirrups."

Tiffany did as she was told. Oh my God! I'm pregnant! I can't have this baby! I don't want this baby! Whose fuckin' baby is it anyway? If it's Mark I don't wanna mess up his college life. If it's Buffalo's at least I have a piece of him for the rest of my life. What the hell was I thinking about not using condoms with them?!? This exam hurts! The fuck is she sticking up me?

After the appointment Tiffany went straight to Jay's garage. Hazel and Jay were in the middle of a meeting with Victor and a new client looking to expand. "Tiffany hey baby how are you?" Victor greets Tiffany with a hug and kiss. "Hey Vick. Who's this?" Tiffany points to the new client. He looked to be in his twenties, not attractive at all, but he dressed well.

"This is Cole. He's from Ohio. He's been buying from me for two years now. He wants to join the Philly crew." Victor explains.

Cole gets up from his chair to properly greet Tiffany.

"How are you doing? I'm Cole. I hear you the one to have watching a nigga back in the streets Tiffany." Tiffany looks him up and down.

"Oh that's what you heard?"

"Yup. I may need you to do a job..once I get Jay's blessings of course."

"Aight. Jay when you finish your meeting. I need to speak with you. I'm gonna go to the Chinese store."

"Okay. We are wrapping up."

Tiffany ordered everything from fried rice to pizza rolls. I was truly in denial to think I wasn't having a baby. I've been eating like crazy! I haven't gained weight though. She hurried back to the garage eating a pizza roll along the way. Victor and Cole were gone. Hazel and Jay sat in the office discussing Cole. "Can we trust him?" Hazel asked Jay.

"Fuck trust Haze. He got a whole other state we can fuck with! He acts up, we kill him and take his soldiers!" Jay shakes his head at Hazel for asking about trust. He notices Tiffany standing in the door eating like a pig.

"Sit down Tiffany! You act like you're starving!" Jay yells while lighting a blunt.

"I need to tell y'all something..." Tiffany explains in between forks full of fried rice.

"What? Did you buy all the fuckin' food? You bring us any?"

"Shut the fuck up Jay! I'm pregnant."

Hazel and Jay stare at each other.

"Have your baby Tiffany." Hazel states.

"I'm not sure... I mean I wanna and I don't."

"But you would have a piece of Buffalo..." Hazel walks over and hugs Tiffany.

" Buffalo...Yeah.. maybe!"

"You fucked the ball player didn't you?!?" Jay exclaims and gets up out of his chair.

"I fuckin' knew it! Tiffany what the fuck? You got a job yo Cole paying ten large on some Cleveland nigga! He wants you on it!" Jay gets in Tiffany's face. Tiffany gets up and pushes Jay. "Don't start your shit Jay! I can still do my job! I don't know if I'm having the baby any damn way okay?"

"Yeah you say that now! I don't wanna hear shit Tiffany! You and Hazel are my top shooters and now you're pregnant! Do the Cole job then that's it! You on break until either you have the baby or get an abortion!"

"Fuck you Jay! You ain't Daddy! What do I need to do for the Cole job?"

Hazel interrupts the siblings arguing.

"Jay, please calm down. Tiffany don't get a abortion. You will regret it like me. I got pregnant before working for Skip. I sometimes wonder how I would be if I kept my baby. I mean the game is the game... but you can work around it. We would never let anything happen to you, Tiffany."

"Naw I wouldn't Tiff! I'm just...damn you pregnant?" Jay is trying to wrap his mind around his sister having a baby.

Tiffany sits back down at the table to finish eating her food before the argument.

"Alright y'all I'll keep it. I still want that Cleveland job. I wanna work until I start showing...me and the baby are gonna need all the money we can get."

Tiffany

December 1998

Being pregnant is a bitch! I mean it's cool to eat whatever you want but that morning sickness and constant peeing has me ready to jump out the window! Janell has been so helpful in my time of need. I'm still able to get around and drop niggas, I need mad massages after. Janell gives the best massages. Everything is tender or sore, especially my tits. That Cleveland job was an easy ten grand I could've killed him with my eyes closed. His whole crew was there and didn't shoot back. Well I mean what would they have shot at? I killed his corny ass from the top floor of an abandoned house across from his favorite bar. The Cleveland cat came out so drunk with some white girl. I took three shots one hit his truck, the second hit his shoulder, and the last shot went straight to the side of his dome. The white chick screamed and ran, his crew ran out the bar and saw him laid out in the street. I was in the wind. Now my last job really tired me out. This deed was also contracted through Cole. This fat nigga in Delaware...he could run. I caught him in the early morning around four, he was leaving his stash house. He was a big guy about six foot and probably three hundred pounds. I shot him in the back and he took off running! I couldn't believe it... I started running after him. Once I gathered myself I was able to get in a decent range to shoot him in the legs and finished him off with a head shot up close. It was a good thing I parked two blocks away from where he was running towards or else I would've been in a shootout. I heard his soldiers as I ran to my car. I'm gonna take a break from contract jobs until after the baby is born. I'm still running my stash house because that's easy.

Mark and I have been talking a lot more on the phone. I didn't tell him I'm pregnant yet. We are going to spend the weekend together at a hotel by the airport. I'm going to pick him up from the train station in an hour. All I have done so far is mention that I lost a close friend. That's what I told him Buffalo was to me. Tonight I plan on telling Mark about Buffalo and that I'm pregnant. Especially since it's a chance the baby is his. Jay really does not care for Mark. He actually told me he hopes the baby is Buffalo's! Jay said it would be 'a real nigga baby.' He thinks Mark is soft and a player. I can't argue with him on it, Mark has played me in the past. I don't know why I can't let him go. At this point what does it matter? I'm possibly carrying his child. He's been doing great with playing college ball. One day I will go to a game.

Tiffany pulled up to the train station, Mark was standing at the door waiting patiently. He was amazed at the car Tiffany was driving. "Yo, Tiffany! You drive a Lexus? This is your car?" Mark hops in the car happily.

"Yeah, one of my cars. I got my people to get us this room for the weekend at a hotel by the airport."

"Cool. Do they have a pool?"

"Yeah they do, I think."

"Yes!" Mark kisses Tiffany on the cheek. The whole ride to the hotel Mark tells Tiffany about his classes and professors. Tiffany listens and nods her head. Mark's life is so much different than my own. Do I really want to tell him I'm pregnant? Get it together Tiffany you didn't do this alone! Just be grateful that Buffalo isn't alive...

The hotel room was so luxurious with a king size bed. Mark dropped his bags, took his shoes, and started jumping on the bed. Tiffany laughed at his childish behavior.

"Come on Tiff!"

"Okay." Tiffany joined him jumping on the bed. This is fun. Mark looks so happy. This is fun but it's making me nauseous. Tiffany stops jumping on the bed.

"I'm hungry, you wanna order room service?" Tiffany asked while looking at the menu on the nightstand.

"Sure. I'm glad we are doing this. I miss you so much. I want you to come to the dorm and see me play. The coach said I have a real shot at the pros! Tiff?!"

Tiffany was lost in the food menu she barely heard a word Mark was saying.

"Yes...Mark I'm definitely gonna do that. Look at this menu, they have everything!"

Mark takes the menu from Tiffany. He figures out what he wants.

"Okay I'm ready to order."

"Cool. I'll call...hello...yes I need to place an order to room 1111. A cheese burger platter with everything, the nachos with cheese, chicken finger platter with honey mustard and barbecue sauce, extra fries, two Pepsi's, and a garden salad with blue cheese dressing. Thank you."

"Damn!!! You're hungry!!! I wasn't gonna say anything but you look like you gained weight."

"Yeah a little. I know it's stress…anyway let's watch television while we wait for the food."

Mark and Tiffany watched Martin reruns holding each other. Room service came in and Mark watched Tiffany pig out on the burger and nachos. All he wanted was chicken fingers.

"Tiffany what happened to your friend you said you lost?"

"He was killed…you want some nachos?"

"Sure…thanks. Do you still hang with Janell and Keke? You haven't spoken about them in a while."

"Janell yes…Keke is dead, it was on the news."

"What?!? I don't watch the news. Oh my God, how did she die?"

"Her boyfriend stabbed her up and put her body on my aunt's steps in a bag."

"Tiffany I'm so sorry! How's your aunt?" Mark hugs Tiffany while she shoving fries down her throat.

"My aunt I guess is making it. Keke was so fucked up…she had a son too…I'm okay though Mark."

Mark starts kissing Tiffany on her back and shoulders. Tiffany stops eating her food to kiss Mark back. "I want a brownie and ice cream! You want dessert?"

"Yeah the same thing. "

Tiffany got back on the phone to call room service. Then she proceeded to eat her feast, Mark touched Tiffany's breast but she didn't rejoin him. Instead she continued to eat. "Once I'm finished eating baby I promise." Tiffany kisses Mark on the lips.

The first night in the hotel with Mark was beautiful. I put his ass to sleep. Not to mention that I ate well. I'm not telling Mark I'm pregnant right now. I can't do it... I will but just not this time.

In the morning the two love birds went downstairs to breakfast. Mark watched Tiffany devour three pancakes, a cheese omelet, grits, and toast. "Do you ever think about going to talk to a doctor about your depression instead of eating?"

"No... I will be fine Mark...do you still see a doctor?"

"I did for a while before I graduated high school. I don't want to take meds though. I hate how they make me feel. I love you and I want you to get better."

Tiffany continues to stuff her face with pancakes. "I love you too...I'm fine really."

As promised Tiffany took Mark to the pool. Tiffany wore a one piece purple bathing suit she didn't want her pregnancy to show. Mark did about five laps across the entire pool. Tiffany stayed at four feet. "Tiffany you're not gonna swim?"

"I don't know how."

"I'll teach you."

Mark teaches Tiffany how to swim. She really didn't want to get her hair wet. He insisted that she learn to at least doggy paddle. Which Tiffany mastered with no problem. She almost felt like she didn't have a care in the world. Until she thought she felt the baby kicking. Wow this is really happening to me. I'm really going to be a mother! I won't be like that no good bitch Brenda, I promise.

After being in the pool for an hour they returned back to the room. Tiffany happily ordered more room service. Mark sat on the edge of the bed. "Tiffany the last time I saw you...you had a gun."

"Yeah. I have guns."

"I try to ignore the fact that you drive a fancy car, wear diamonds, and carry weapons. Is that why we are going slow? Because you're into some street stuff?"

"Mark...Yeah. I need you to understand."

"Why don't you quit?"

"It's not simple...can we enjoy our time together?"

Mark didn't respond, instead he laid back on the bed and closed his eyes. Thinking back on the night he was an innocent bystander and was shot. I don't want Tiffany to die.

"Tiffany, remember when I got shot?"

"Yeah."

"Did you get shot? I see the scar on your shoulder?"

"Mark! Please!"

Room service arrived right on time. Mark answers the door. The rest of the day was spent in silence unless Tiffany ordered room service. That night Mark just held Tiffany in her sleep. Tears ran down his eyes in his sleep. He put his hands on Tiffany's stomach and felt a strange light kick. He was startled by it at first. Mark decided to rub his hands across her stomach. The baby made light movements. She's having a baby! That's why she's been eating so much. How could I have been so stupid? Is this my baby? Is this why Tiffany wanted to take me away? Oh my God I'm gonna be a dad! Should I wake her up? No let her sleep.

Tiffany was wondering why she woke to Mark being so loving. He insisted on ordering breakfast through room service. "We can stay right here. You rest beautiful. Go ahead and order breakfast first. Then I need to tell you something important." Mark smiles and waits for Tiffany to order breakfast. What the hell is Mark up to? Tiffany gives Mark the side eye while on the phone. "Okay Mark What is it now?"

"I felt the baby last night while you were sleeping. Is it my baby? I will do whatever I have to do for my child. I thought about it. I'll quit school and go get a job. I want you to stop being in the streets." Tiffany listened to Mark talk of dumping his future down the drain. I can't allow him to ruin his life for me. "It's not yours Mark...that's what I wanted to tell you. Before my friend was killed we had sex." Mark's face swelled up with sadness and anger. "Tiffany! You cheated on me! How could you!" Mark gets up from the bed. He looks around the room and grabs the remote control. Mark throws it at the mirror, the mirror cracks. "Mark, please calm down! Don't break shit okay! You've cheated plenty!"

"Shut up!" Mark yells as he begins punching the wall. Tiffany gets up to stop Mark from acting out. Mark falls to the floor with tears in his eyes. "I never got anyone pregnant! I thought you loved me Tiffany!"

"Mark...Let's go. I'm gonna take you home. I don't want to fuck your life up anymore. I'm sorry."

Mark wiped his tears from his cheeks. He looks up at Tiffany at first he hesitates to get up from the floor. "Alright Tiffany. Can you drop me off at the bus? You don't have to take me home. I told my uncle you and I was back together...he can't see you pregnant,"

"Mark...I'm taking you home. I just won't come in."

"Fine..."

"Mark...I love you. I never meant to hurt you. If you hate me now I understand...my life is my life..."

"I see that so clearly now Tiffany." Mark and Tiffany pack their bags and leave the hotel room together, the entire ride to Mark's house was silent. When Mark got out of the car neither one of them said anything to each other.

May 1, 1999

My pregnancy went by really fast. I'm due basically any day now. This baby has given me huge breasts and thighs. The only time I go outside is to see the doctor or go eat. Hazel's in charge of my stash house, since I started showing. We agreed it was best to keep my pregnancy a secret to the soldiers who don't know me like that. I mean they know I'm their boss and under Jay, that's all. Hazel, Janell, and Tara have been by my side. Janell told Tara I was pregnant because she wouldn't stop asking Janell about me. Tara was working at our whore house in North Philly under Mike but got sent over to Janell's in West. Tara was a hot head. She beat up two of the girls in North Philly with her Stiletto shoe. Before Buffalo died he had her at our whore house in Southwest Philly things got crazy there for Tara too. She bust a guy upside the head with a beer bottle. In Tara's defense the guy shorted her fifty dollars and the girls in North stole out her purse. Mike keeps telling her if she has any problems, tell him but Tara ain't hearing that. All three girls take turns going with me to my doctor's appointment. They all argue over who's going to be the godmother of my baby. Of course it's going to be my best friend Janell. I purposely don't know what I'm having. I want to be surprised.

For the past couple of weeks someone has been playing on my cell phone. Every time I go to answer the phone whoever is on the other line would hang on me. The numbers are random too. Hazel tells me not to sweat it but I don't like that someone is fuckin' with me and I can't address them. I'm thinking of just getting another phone to alleviate the bull. Mark was the first person who came to mind who could possibly be playing on my phone. The numbers that come up are local. Since that day in the hotel I haven't heard from Mark. I started to reach out to him during his spring break but the girls told me not to. I made up my mind that if it is Mark's child I'm not going to ruin his life. I will take care of the baby alone. One of his games I saw on television and he truly has what it takes to be a pro for the NBA. The last thing I need is for him to regret his life the way my father did. I didn't purposely get pregnant, we just weren't thinking. If it's Buffalo's baby I know it would make the gang happy and he would inherit what we have laid out especially if it's a boy. Mike wasn't mad at me when I told him about me sleeping with Mark. Mike said he understood that Buffalo changed and whatever happened was our personal business. Jay stayed in New York for a couple months and then he went down south. Jay stayed in Virginia for a week. He peaked in on Vanessa. He didn't approach her though. Vanessa is happy with her new life. Jay's name has travelled fast and all the way to South Carolina at that. His empire that he had planned out since eleven is really a dream come true, for Jay. He started making light investments like Victor advised. He put in on opening a little bar in Harlem. Hazel said she and Jay are finally having sex. He still did not tell Hazel how old he is but he knew he couldn't hold back from that part of their relationship any longer.

I went to visit my Daddy once since being pregnant. It was the hardest thing I have done in my life so far. He cried the majority of the visit. I almost cried too but I stayed strong. I promised him a high school education and I failed him. Well after I have the baby I'll see about a GED. I told him school just isn't for me. He thinks he has failed me as a father. I assured him that's not the case. I did tell him that Buffalo died and not to worry about me. I'm safe. He told me that my aunt Pat wrote to him about Keke being murdered. She said that raising Devin has helped her cope with all her losses.

My Dad asked me a question that I never thought he would ask and I had to lie. He said "Tiffany is Little John working for this Jay guy that's been helping me? I won't get mad...I just need to know is Little John still alive?"

I told him "Daddy I don't know where Little John is."

If I told Daddy that Jay is Little John...he may try to break out of prison. The next time I go see Daddy will be when the baby is at least six months. I also told Daddy that. We hugged at the end of the visit and took a nice picture.

Tiffany got up to do her daily stretches and light exercise. Her goal was to get back in shape immediately after the baby came out. Tiffany decided on breastfeeding for a while too. As much as she is excited to be a mother she also couldn't wait to get back on the street. There's more money to be made and ungrateful niggas that need to be laid to rest. Tara came over to join her in her workout. Every time Tiffany sees Tara her palms get sweaty and her heart skips a beat. Tara hugs Tiffany then bends over to kiss Tiffany's stomach. The baby starts jumping immediately. "Aww I hope it's a girl!" Tara exclaims.

"I want to be surprised...hmmm however secretly I wouldn't mind a boy."

"For real!"

"Yup. Now let's get these squats going."

Tiffany uses her living room wall for support as she does her squats. On her third squat Tiffany feels a gush of fluid flowing down her legs. "What the fuck!" Tiffany yelled.

Tara looks down and gets excited. "Tiffany, your water broke! The baby is coming!"

Tiffany and Tara leave the apartment quickly. Tiffany starts having contractions back to back. "Tara this hurts!!! Aaahh! I want this baby out!!! I gotta call Janell and Hazel!"

"Tiffany, take breaths! I'll call them when we get to the hospital." Tara rubs Tiffany's hand.

The maternity team rushed Tiffany for delivery. She had dilated six centimeters. In the midst of Tiffany's scream and gripping Tara's hand, Tara managed to call Janell.

One hour later Tiffany gives birth to a beautiful healthy baby girl. She was seven pounds and five ounces. Tiffany gave birth all natural with no drugs. When Tiffany looked at her darling little girl her face reminded her of Snoopy. The baby's cheeks were puffy and her eyes kind of beady.

" Look at Snoopy." Tiffany tells Hazel, Janell, and Tara. They all laughed. Tiffany holds her daughter tight. I won't ever do you how my mama did me, Tiffany starts to think of Brenda. How unloving and disgusting Brenda was towards all three of them. The nurses came in and took Snoopy for testing. "Bring my baby back in one piece!" Tiffany tells the nurse.

"Tiffany the baby will be fine!" Janell assures Tiffany.

"Shut up! I'm so hungry! Somebody go get me a hoagie please."

"I'll go...that means you want me to go around to a corner store?" Janell asked.

"Duh, Janell. We ain't far away." Tiffany snaps. Janell gives Tiffany the finger and takes Hazel's car keys.

"I'm telling the doctor we are leaving tomorrow." Tiffany states.

"Tiff you crazy!" Hazel laughs.

"Watch. They better hurry up with my baby. I'm leaving tomorrow morning."

"They probably will let you..." Tara chimes in.

"I know they are."

Moment of Truth

July 1999

Snoopy is such a good baby. She looks like Mark at times, sometimes I want to call him, and other times I know it's best to leave him be. I found out that it was my Aunt Pat calling my phone. Janell thought that she was helping me with family issues by giving aunt Pat my number. She went by there to check on them behind my back. I was furious at first but Janell is someone you can't stay mad at. Aunt Pat was calling from bars or work. All she wanted was to hear my voice. Janell didn't tell her I was having a baby. I didn't tell her either. The less she knows about me the better. Even though I'm sure by now she may know because of Daddy. He sent me a letter asking about the baby. Jay stays with me some nights to spend time with Snoopy. He was mad that Snoopy wasn't Buffalo's baby. Jay wants me to tell Mark, I just can't. One day I will. Maybe.

Victor asked to meet with Jay and I in private at the halfway point. I didn't want to bring Snoopy out in the heat so I left her with Janell. Victor says this meeting is urgent. So of course Jay is strapped up and heated. I'm playing it cool with my strap though. When we got out of the truck Victor was in his car smoking a cigar pacing. Jay and I looked at each other before walking over to Victor.

"What's up Vick?" Jay asked.

"Come sit with me family." Victor takes a seat on the bench, Tiffany and Jay sit down next to him.

"Now you know I spent time down south with Star and Zora until things cooled off up here. What I didn't tell you is where…"

"Okay…so where is Vick?" Jay asked, getting impatient.

"We stayed with Mabel and Sunny."

"Our grandma?" Tiffany asked.

"Yeah…"

"So?" Tiffany states sucking her teeth.

"Your grandma is sick…she's dying and Star said we gotta go back down south. We can't find Brenda and Mabel is requesting for Tiffany."

"She hates me! How does she know anything about me?"

"Star told her I would use my connections to find you. They don't know anything about you Tiffany. Mabel has cancer and Sunny called today and said they are giving her one month to live."

"Good now she can join her rapist ass son in hell!" Tiffany yells.

"Tiffany, I have to ask you to come with me. I promised Star... I never break my promises to her. If you don't like it after we get there I'll bring you back home."

"Promise me like you promised Star! If it wasn't for you being who you are to Jay. I would say hell no and not think twice about it!"

"Of all the connects mine turns out to be my big cousin.." Jay shakes his head.

"Fate." Victor tells Jay placing his hand on Jay's shoulder.

"Some fate...Tiffany we gotta honor this. Vick when are y'all leaving?"

"Tomorrow morning four I think. So I will be in Philly to get you and the baby by six."

"Damn Vick!" Tiffany gets up from the bench to light her black and mild.

"Go home, pack up and get the baby ready. I'm taking my truck. There will be plenty of room for you. You will finally meet your cousin Zora."

"Cool Vick. Jay let's go."

On the way back home Jay just stayed to himself listening to Jay-Z. Tiffany didn't want a quiet ride. "Jay what the fuck could she want me for?"

"I don't know Tiffany but it's a done deal. Old bitch acts up and you kill her. Shit put a pillow over her face."

"I can't stand you Jay!"

Tiffany hurried up to pack up whatever she thought she would need to take down south. Janell watched her going from draw to draw. Snoopy laid comfortably in her car seat making bubbles.

"Tiffany, did you tell Aunt Pat?"

"No. I don't truly care to go to Janell! If it wasn't for Vick honoring a request I wouldn't be going and if she died I guess Aunt Pat would call me from a bar!"

Janell laughs at Tiffany. She sits next to Snoopy's car seat.

"You always think something is funny!" Tiffany starts throwing clothes all over the floor.

"Tiffany, relax! She may have something for you."

"Like what some Newports? She ain't shit! She threw her life away! Just like Brenda! I'm nothing like them! I could never treat my Snoopy the way I was treated! Only my Daddy loves me out of my so-called parents."

"Tiffany let out all that now and be a bad bitch when you get down south. You understand? Don't give them any of these emotions. You go and show your family down south how much you don't need them."

"Yeah you're right…because I don't. Ain't nobody ever come take me or Little John and Vanessa for a summer visit! Only family that tried was Aunt Pat and now she all fucked up too. They ain't gonna help her or come to Keke's funeral! You're right Janell. I'm only doing this Victor."

The entire evening was going by slowly. Tiffany checked on her stash house and then met up with Jay at the garage. "Today was so so we only made fifteen grand. Chris said no one is stealing. He had to punch a feen in the face today but that was all. Chris, I like him. He's loyal."

"After this Carolina trip…Cole wants you again."

"Oh yeah?"

"Yup this time it's personal and he doesn't want it to look like it came from him."

"Cole man…what's his deal?"

"He is taking over his city and a few others out there. You know he partnered up with us and got some spots out here Delaware and New York. He's a good investment. His soldiers are right too. It's just that he likes your style."

"Style huh?" Tiffany sits down at the desk and puts her feet up.

"Yeah you know you are an out of town hitter. Word is getting around too, niggas don't believe it's a female doing it like this."

Tiffany smiles at Jay and then lights her blunt.

"Aight Jay I gotta get back in and relieve Janell from Snoopy. She is staying at the apartment while I'm gone just so you know."

Meeting Star and Zora was awkward at first. I had to pretend like I just met Vick. Star asked me all these questions about my whereabouts. I played it cool and told them I live with Janell. Star was careful not to mention Todd. Zora at first just glanced at me and Snoopy. The more Star and I talked I noticed she changed her disposition. Zora told me about being in Philly staying in the basement with Brenda and then going to fight my aunt Divine. I can't believe how easy it is for Brenda to drag people into her foolishness and drama. Zora comes off like she's down for whatever. Star just looks carefree as long as she can go shopping and Victor takes care of them. Her life is good. I bet

Brenda was jealous of Star and Victor. It's funny how Brenda never brought us around them or invited them to visit us, but Brenda kept her own private relationships with a lot of family members. When there were family reunions or dinners only Brenda and Mabel would attend most of the time. My dad would be left home with us. If there was any family coming around our house it was for Brenda's own agenda. I wonder if she's dead or overdosed somewhere since no one can find her. Snoopy was doing well during this road trip. She only cried for my milk once. I made sure to pump enough bottles for the ride and I put some cereal to keep her full longer.

The air down south felt thick like on Earth hell. The air conditioner was barely keeping us cool the rest of the ride. The house we arrived at is where Grandma Mabel grew up, Star told me. The house was beautiful surrounded by grass and a dirt road. I wonder what would have been if we lived here instead. I mean the house is so big. It's a three story house with a big porch. On the porch was a white rocking chair that I'm sure Mabel was rocking her fat ass on. We just walked into the house and the door wasn't locked. A place where they don't lock doors! I mean they aren't scared that someone would rob them? Uncle Sunny was in the kitchen making iced tea. In the living room were people I had never seen before but Star and Victor greeted them with love. I guess that's family. I took a seat and removed Snoopy from her car seat. "What a prudy baby!" The woman sitting beside me says. I couldn't quite understand her so I just said "thanks."

"Are you Brenda's daughter?"

"I guess. Who are you?"

" I'm yo cousin' Jessie."

"Ok."

"We always wanted to meet y'all but we don't like Philadelphia. We asked Brenda to bring y'all down here but she never did."

"Oh...ok." Tiffany sees Uncle Sunny walk in the living room.

"Tiffany."

"Uncle Sunny."

"I called Patricia but I don't think she is coming down. Nobody said you had a baby. Are those real diamonds?"

"Yup."

"Gertrude is gonna be starting supper soon. If you're hungry now there's some cake and iced tea." Uncle Sunny goes upstairs.

Zora turns on the television to break the silence. Tiffany sees that Aunt Pat is calling her from her house number finally.

Tiffany answers and walks out to the porch. "Yes Aunt Pat?"

"You went down there to see Mabel?"

"I didn't want to but yes."

"I'm not coming fuck all of them! If she dies, she dies! None of them were there for me and now that Mabel is dying I'm supposed to drop my life for them? Naw!"

"I understand Aunt Pat...how are the boys?"

"Good. I gotta go...be strong Tiffany...one day I want to see you."

"We will see. Take care Aunt Pat." Tiffany hangs up the phone and returns to the living room.

Uncle Sunny comes back downstairs. "Tiffany, you can go up."

Tiffany looks at everyone before going upstairs, she holds onto Snoopy tight.

"Everything is gonna be fine." Star assures Tiffany. Tiffany doesn't say a word.

Even the upstairs was huge. Tiffany counted four bedrooms before finding Mabel's room.

When Tiffany opens the door she sees a woman that resembles her Grandma Mabel.

"Grandma Mabel?"

"Yeah. I know you used to see my fat ass but that cancer is eating me up." Mabel takes a deep breath after making her statement. Even her voice was different.

"You wanted to see me?"

"Yes...that your...baby?"

"Yes. She's a few months old."

"She's...beautiful. Sit...down Tiffany."

Tiffany sits down. Snoopy starts to blow bubbles.

"Now...I know we didn't have the best relationship... I know I was a terrible grandmother... I realized as time went on that my daughter...I created that monster..."

Mabel takes deep breaths.

"I should've protected you... I knew Todd had a problem...he has been...that way since he was a boy...his daddy abused him...and I caught the bass player from...his fathers band molesting him... I was...just so caught... up in my life... I...thought I was doing my best."

Tiffany interrupts Mabel. "Was the bass player a man?"

"No...a woman...she had been getting high with his father...and then went and abused my boy...I'm so sorry...Tiffany... I asked Brenda if he ever touched her...she said...no...but I don't believe her...please...forgive me..." Mabel begins to struggle for air gasping taking deep breaths. Tiffany just watches Mabel for a few seconds before screaming for help. Uncle Sunny and Victor arrive in the room to see Mabel gone. Tiffany forced tears down her eyes. I don't want them to know that I'm happy that bitch is dead. Oh you sorry on your death bed? I would be sorry to! The rest of the family came into the room and prayed over Mabel's body. Tiffany didn't join in on the prayers. She sat in the hallway holding Snoopy in a daze. Tiffany found herself back in her room with Todd forcing her to give him oral sex. She sees his body fall on her again, tasting his blood, and her father pointing the gun at Mabel. He should've killed you then.

Who has been reading Tiffany's Diaries

May 2018

Jada (Snoopy)

Jada finally worked up the nerve to go into her mothers secret storage unit in Southwest Philly. The storage unit was under Jada's name. Jada just turned nineteen a week ago. For her birthday she had a big party given to her by Uncle John, Aunt Janell, and Tara. They rented a hall in west Philly with a DJ and catered food. During the party all she could think of is her mother. She wanted to feel her mother again. She also was secretly looking for clues. Inside the unit she found childhood toys and stuffed animals. Jada's first pair of walking shoes and a chess set. The chess was big, beautiful, silver, and shiny. She wanted to open it but couldn't find a key in the unit. Jada decided to haul it to her mothers house instead.. Tiffany was so secretive, Jada thought. Once she got to Tiffany's house Jada ran upstairs to her mothers room to find the key. She searched all over the dressers. Nothing. Jada had almost given up on looking in her mothers secret pretty chess. It's so heavy I hope it's money. Jada had decided to go inside her old bedroom. On the dresser were pictures of her and Tiffany. Jada had taken the pictures herself with a camera Mark brought for her birthday one year. My mom did love me. She gave me everything she never had. On her night stand she noticed two tiny keys. They were not identical but on the same key ring. Hmmm. Jada looked and thought couldn't be. Did she leave this here for me? Nobody else can get in here but me. Jada has not been to their west Philadelphia home since the murder. She had been staying at the apartment downtown with Tara.

Jada drags the chess upstairs to her mothers room. Everything still looks the same. Jada tries the first tiny key and inserts it into the chess lock. That one doesn't work. She tries the last one and it works.

Several hours later...

Jada gets up from the white plush carpet of her deceased mothers room. Tears are flowing uncontrollably down her face. She couldn't believe what she just read about her mother and herself for that matter. Mark is my father!!! Every time I would look him in the eyes I felt like I was looking into my own. Jada looks in the mirror and places a picture of Mark next to her face. I'm a splitting image of Mark. My Pop Pop is in jail for protecting my Mother?!?! My mother was a... Grandma Brenda really is a bitch! Jada looked at the chess set that was full of composition books, letters from her Grandfather in jail and newspaper articles her mother had written and labeled Tiffany's dairy.

Jada laid on her deceased mother's Queen size bed. It still smelled like her. Mommy she thought...Jada begins to think of Tiffany. How she would have reacted by catching Jada in her room reading her diaries. I could hear her voice now "What the hell are you doing?" "These are private Jada! What did I tell you about being so nosy?!?"

Then she thinks of the times she's spent with Mark and his children. All the questions she asked Tiffany about why she doesn't know her dad and who he is. She would always say to me 'Don't worry about who he is, Jada! I love you! I will take care of you...'

Jada laid on the bed and cried herself to sleep.

The Author

Porsche Day was born and raised in Philadelphia.

Day developed a love for writing as a child. Her writing has allowed her to build a career as the erotic Poet "Thick Nubian Goddess". The Diary of a Former Sex Addict series is the first of many hot releases from Day. Day's entrepreneur journey has her fearlessly pursuing acting while building her holistic coaching business.

www.ingramcontent.com/pod-product-compliance
Lightning Source LLC
Chambersburg PA
CBHW060124260626
47160CB00005B/2011